ONLY ONE WINNER

Four stories of murder, deceit and ambition, set against a backdrop of future space colonisation. *Only One Winner* presents four criminals, desperate to strike it rich by holding up a luxury tourist space cruiser. However, internal distrust and animosity threatens to leave them worse off than when they started . . . This, and three other stories exploring human nature in the face of life-threatening situations, question how wise it is to put your faith in strangers, and whether greed ever pays off . . .

E.C. TUBB

ONLY ONE WINNER

Complete and Unabridged

LINFORD
Leicester

First published in Great Britain

First Linford Edition
published 2014

Copyright © 1955, 1957 by E.C. Tubb
Copyright © 2013 by Lisa John

A catalogue record for this book is available
from the British Library.

ISBN 978–1–4448–2014–0

Published by
F. A. Thorpe (Publishing)
Anstey, Leicestershire

Set by Words & Graphics Ltd.
Anstey, Leicestershire
Printed and bound in Great Britain by
T. J. International Ltd., Padstow, Cornwall

This book is printed on acid-free paper

Three men and a woman on a blood-stained trail among the stars. Four people who forgot in the gamble of life there is only one winner.

ONLY ONE WINNER

The candle was Stanson's. He'd made it from a can of vitapaste, shaping the thick grease around a wick of twisted medical gauze. As a candle it was nothing to boast about, but it gave light and a little heat and it was company of a sort.

Learhy sat on a box and stared at it. His eyes reflected the flame, glistening as it flared, dulling as it died. Hard eyes in a hard face. A craggy, unhandsome face of planes and hollows and deep-graved lines. It matched his body, a tough, lumpy body without grace but with a crude, animal strength. He cupped his chin, his elbows resting on his knees and his hands were like the rest of him, scarred and battered by violence.

The tiny flame guttered and almost died. Learhy tensed, his muscles bunching, then forced himself to relax as the light brightened. Impurities in the grease; too high a water content for steady

3

burning even here where there was no wind, no draught, no stirring of the air to disturb the flame. Vitapaste made a poor fuel, but Stanson had said that the candle would burn until there was nothing left to give it life. And Stanson had known what he was talking about.

Learhy turned his eyes to where he rested, his back against the piled boxes, his legs extended over the smooth metal. Stanson, the clever one. The one who had tried to be just a little too clever. His eyes were open and his lips twisted into what could have been a grin. In the fitful light both lips and eyes seemed to have movement so that he trembled on the verge of speech and his eyes turned from Learhy towards the candle, from the candle towards Learhy. But it was all a trick of the light. Stanson could neither speak nor see. Stanson was lucky. Stanson was dead.

Learhy ignored him and concentrated on the candle. He stared at it until it filled his vision. A flickering point of light ringed with a yellow nimbus, the whole edged with black. A dancing mote of *brilliance hovering above a sagging cylinder of grey. A speck of light and warmth in an infinity of dark and cold. He couldn't stop looking at it.*

It measured his life.

★　★　★

The idea had been crazy from the start. Stanson had conceived it, nurtured it, given it final birth. Stanson with the cruel mouth and the shrewd eyes, the thin body and the agile mind. Stanson, who was serving the last month of his term and who shared a cell in Block A with Learhy.

It wasn't a comfortable cell, not by modern standards. It held a couple of bunks, toilet facilities, an outsized calendar and a thin row of books. It was big enough to move around in yet too small for exercise. It was a coop, nothing more, a cage in which to keep the unwanted. Against one wall a TV set flared in light and colour, served by the master-set within the prison.

'Nice programme.' Stanson stared

appreciatively at the screen. The programme, as usual, concerned itself with
women who worried more about their
measurements than about their modesty.
Learhy didn't comment. He lay on the
top bunk, his eyes closed, his head
pressing hard against his pillow. He was
sweating a little.

'Some dames!' Stanson smacked his
lips. 'Makes a man glad to be alive.'

'Does it?' Learhy opened his eyes and
lifted himself on one elbow. He didn't
look at the screen. 'How about turning
that thing off?'

'The telly? Why?'

'Because I said so.' Learhy slipped from
the bunk with a sudden release of energy.
He reached the set and punched the
button all in one smooth motion. Silence
closed around them, but not for long.
Through the air came the hint of music,
the echoes of laughter, the transmitted
sounds from the other TV sets, one to a
cell, five hundred in the block, all
operating at full pressure.

Learhy sagged and pressed his hands
over his ears.

Torture is sometimes unintentional. The people who had made it their business to provide comforts for the prisoners would have been insulted and hurt had anyone called them sadists, yet that is what they were. How better can you torture a man than by cooping him up, denying him a natural life, and then showing him everything that he is missing? Books weren't too bad; they offered escape into an unreal world, but there was nothing unreal about the TV sets. They pictured real men and women, real comforts, a real way of life. And it was almost impossible to turn them off. Boredom was too great for any man to deliberately deny himself distraction.

Stanson switched on the screen. 'Relax,' he warned. 'You're not acting natural.' He glanced at the spy-mike set in the roof. 'Watch yourself or they'll throw you in Psycho and keep you there until you rot.'

'Thanks for nothing.'

'If that's what you want, then go ahead.' Stanson shrugged. 'Seems stupid to me though. You'll be out of the can soon, and then the world's yours.'

'Sure.' Learhy was ironic.

'I mean it.' Stanson lowered his voice. 'You want that stuff?' His head jerked towards the TV screen. 'Well, you can have it.'

'Me and a couple of million credits,' Learhy agreed. 'You got a spare couple of million?'

'Maybe.' Stanson's eyes were veiled. 'You know Madame Julie's?'

'The dive on Fifty-Eight Avenue? I know it.'

'Meet me there when you get out.'

'Why?'

'I've got an idea,' said Stanson. 'A good idea.'

Learhy didn't know then how crazy it was.

* * *

Madame Julie was fifty years old, and looked it. She was a woman to whom love and credits were one and the same thing, and charity didn't exist. She looked at Learhy, read his immediate past and

8

probable future and jerked her head towards the door.

'On your way, mister. No handouts.'

'I'm not looking for a handout.' Learhy crushed his quick anger. 'I'm looking for a friend.' He stepped forward towards the bar, then stopped as she stepped in front of him.

'No trouble,' she said softly. 'Try anything and you'll regret it.'

'I want no trouble. I want a drink.' He misread her expression. 'I can pay for it.'

'Sure you can. You can pay for one, maybe two, and then what? Then you get a little drunk and start an argument.'

'On two drinks?'

'You're a con,' she said. 'You're not used to drinking. With a couple under your belt you'll be feeling high. You'll start annoying the girls, and that'll annoy the customers. For the profit from a couple of drinks it just isn't worth it.'

Behind her, the bar door swung open, releasing a mingled odour of whisky, cigarette smoke and perfume. A jukebox vied with female laughter in artificial sound. A burly spacer came towards them. He was more than a little drunk and was spoiling for a fight.

'What kind of a joint is this?' he demanded. 'A guy spends all his coin and then gets the thumbs down sign from a cheap dame who . . . '

'Watch your mouth, mister!' Julie said sharply. 'If you don't like the rules, you don't have to play.'

He said something he'd learned in the gutter, then repeated it with elaborations. Learhy, not really caring, but seizing his opportunity, stepped forward, his right fist a fast-moving blur. The spacer grunted, looked foolish, then sagged at the knees. Learhy caught him as he fell.

'Nice work,' said Julie. She hadn't moved. 'Maybe I could use you.'

'You've got your own bouncers.' Learhy let the spacer fall. 'What happens next?'

'We put him on ice until he recovers. Then we wipe his nose, give him a drink and send him on his way.' She shrugged, a slight movement of the shoulders. 'No percentage in rolling him; there's more profit in the good rep he'll give the joint.'

Her fingers fumbled in a belt-bag. 'Here. Something for your trouble.'

'Thanks.' He took the money. 'Now to business. You know Stanson?'

'Jack Stanson?' Her eyes grew wary. 'Maybe. Why?'

'I'm looking for him. He said for me to meet him here.'

'Why didn't you say that before?' She looked at him, examining his face, body and eyes. 'Where did you meet?'

'Queensbrough, Block A, name of Learhy. He knows me.'

'It's your grief if he doesn't.' She gestured towards the stairs. 'Wait in number eighteen. Don't go straying.'

'Can't I wait in the bar?'

'You'll wait where I tell you. I don't want con-smell upsetting the customers. Anything you want?'

'Nothing I can't pay for.' Learhy pushed past her towards the stairs. 'Get word to Stanson and tell him not to keep me waiting.'

★ ★ ★

11

He waited an hour in a dingy room containing a bed, washbasin, a faded carpet, a wardrobe, empty, and very little else. He killed time by leafing through a heap of tattered magazines and listening to the thunder of jets from the nearby rocket port. He tried to catch a glimpse of the spaceships, but the window opened onto an airshaft and it was impossible to see the sky. From below came the faint sounds of revelry as the joint warmed up for the night. At the end of an hour he ran out of patience and was heading towards the door when Stanson arrived. He wasn't alone.

'Glad you made it,' he said 'This is Klien. Klien, meet Learhy. We went to the same school.'

'Just out?' Klien was a pudgy, heavy-set man with bloodshot eyes and a haunted expression. His clothes were poor and his breath stank of whisky. He held out a clammy hand. 'How long were you in?'

'Too long.' Learhy dropped the hand.

Stanson pushed the pudgy man towards the door. 'Now that you've met, you'd better get sociable. Go down to the bar and collect a couple of bottles. Tell Julie to put them on my account.' He waited until they were alone. 'Don't make a snap judgment, Learhy. Klien is one of the best.'

'The best of what?'

'He's a good man.' Stanson produced cigarettes, offered one to Learhy, and lit them both. He lit them with an inlaid gas lighter which must have cost the best part of a month's wages for an average man. His clothes reflected his prosperity. Next to him, Learhy felt shabby and pale. Stanson chuckled, tossing the lighter from hand to hand.

'A week of good eating, some sun-lamp treatment and a new suit will fix you up. Nothing like a coat of tan to get rid of the con-smell.'

'Throw in a trip to the North Pole while you're at it,' said Learhy dryly. 'Nothing like a good vacation to get a man on his feet again.'

'Now you're talking.' Stanson pocketed the lighter. 'There's little a smart man can't get, not if he wants it bad enough.'

'Like Klien?'

'Klien's all right.'

'He's a drunk.' Learhy inhaled, holding the smoke in his lungs before letting it gush from between his lips. 'I don't trust a man who gets his kicks from a bottle.'

'You can trust Klien all the way.'

'I trust no one that far.'

'Maybe you're right, but you can trust Klien as far as you can trust anyone.' Stanson was serious. Learhy shrugged, not wanting to make an issue of it.

'He's still a drunk in my book.'

Klien returned before Stanson could answer. He pushed open the door and marched into the room, a bottle in each hand. He set one down on the table, tore the cork from the other and helped himself to a long drink. He stood, bottle in hand, looking at Learhy. 'I heard what you said.'

'So?'

'So you got it wrong. I drink, yes, but I don't drink to get a lift. I drink to stop getting depressed. There's a difference, you know.'

'Not enough to make it important.' Learhy dropped his cigarette, stepped on

14

it and looked at Stanson. 'You said for me to meet you. I'm here. What happens now?'

'There is a difference,' insisted Klien. 'Most men drink to get a kick, but I'm not like that. I've got to drink to keep normal. If I don't drink then I hit bottom.'

'Shut up.' Learhy didn't feel like swapping philosophy with the pudgy man. 'I'm waiting, Stanson. What do we do now?'

'We talk.' Stanson drew up chairs, tossed his cigarettes on the table and sat down. Klien, after tilting the bottle again, joined him. Learhy stood by his chair.

'Talk?'

'The prelude to action. We talk big, think big and then, when everything's settled, we act big.'

'How big?' Learhy wasn't impressed; he'd heard con-talk before.

'I don't know.' Stanson helped himself to a fresh cigarette. 'How big is big? Ten million? Twenty? You tell me.'

'No.' Learhy sat down and rested his hands on the table. 'You tell me.'

'I'll tell you,' promised Stanson. 'I'll tell you all about it.'

He started and Learhy listened to the great idea. It was crazy; as crazy as the concept of writing with a ball instead of a nib, as stupid as the idea of being able to talk through the air without the aid of wires. It was so crazy that it might even work.

Stanson wanted to steal a spaceship.

* * *

In a world ridden by officialdom, strangled by red tape and clogged by countless forms in triplicate, the forger comes into his own. Men are no longer men, but the papers they carry. The passport, visa, identification slip, travel order, ticket, insurance certificate, tax clearance papers, union card, bank book, health form, they, and a dozen other scraps of paper, all go to prove that the person carrying them is the person they claim him to be. Officials stare at forms, not men. Pass forms, not men, and, if the forms are in order, then they are happy.

Learhy hoped they would stay happy.

He stood in a line of a couple of dozen men and tried to relax as he neared the examining office. Before him, Stanson waited his turn, smoking, despite the notice forbidding it. Behind him, Klien, looking hangdog and harried from lack of whisky, shuffled almost last in line. Learhy didn't turn to look at him. He was playing a part and had to remember to keep in character. He was a worker bound under contract to the waste disposal workings on the Moon. And he had papers to prove it.

Ahead of him a minor Hitler snapped to outraged protest at Stanson's lack of discipline.

'You there! Kill that butt!'

Stanson inhaled, looking everywhere but at the irate official.

'You!' Somewhere the man had picked up some gutterfilth. He used it with relish. Stanson looked startled, dropped the cigarette, trod on it and sheepishly approached the examiner muttering apologies. The examiner swore at him, made some threats as to what would happen if he didn't watch himself, glanced at his papers and passed him through. Learhy relaxed as Stanson passed through the shed and out onto the field. He tightened again as the man before him ran into trouble.

'These papers aren't in order.' The examiner scowled at them. 'They should have been stamped by the tax people.' He threw them back. 'I can't pass you.'

'Why not?' The man wanted to argue. 'If I miss this shuttle I'll be docked or fined for contract breaking. Hell, why should I suffer because some snotty-nosed clerk didn't do his job?'

'I can't pass you.' The examiner was firm, and Learhy realized why Stanson had acted as he did. Divert their attention from the papers to the man and things were that much easier. You can't examine two things at once, not closely, not if you're pressed for time. He tripped over his own feet as he walked to the desk, the papers fluttering from his hand. He picked them up, dusted them, and passed them over.

'Joe Milton,' he babbled. 'Two-year

contract with Atomic Waste Disposals, Inc. Good job, eh?'

'Some people say so.' The examiner riffled the sheaf of documents.

'They told me it was a good job,' insisted Learhy. 'Good food, good pay and plenty of recreation.' He winked. 'I sure could use some of that recreation.'

'First-timer, aren't you?' The examiner was amused. He knew what this man apparently didn't, that working for Waste Disposals was a thin step above working for the devil. Handling radioactive sludge was a job only the desperate would accept. The desperate or the dumb.

'That's right.' Learhy stabbed at the papers with a grimy finger. 'They tell me it's tough, but I'm healthy and can take it. See? On that form there somewhere. See?'

'I see.' The examining officer turned away his head as Learhy breathed into his face. Artificial halitosis was a good inducement not to relish a man's company. The thud of the rubber stamp signalled Learhy to be on his way.

Outside the shed a guard pointed to

where the shuttle-rocket stood waiting. Learhy didn't look for Stanson; he would already be aboard, and he dared not wait for Klien: that would be out of character. Not that he had to worry about Klien. When a man makes three sets of false papers, common sense dictates that he keep the best set for himself.

A crewman guided him to a thin anti-G mattress and clipped him down. The shuttle was small, overloaded with cheap human freight, and the air system needed an overhaul. Lying in the dim, blue-lit darkness, Learhy listened to transmitted sound. A mutter of voices, a curse, a whimper, then the clang of metal as the entry port was sealed and the whine of a siren. Idly he wondered what had happened to the three men whose place they had taken. He didn't wonder for long. The shock of take-off gripped him and left room for nothing but pain.

* * *

There are two ways to leave planet. One is the easy way, a slow and gentle lift using plenty of fuel and taking plenty of time. That was the way the custom trade used with multi-millionaires, the glamour girls, the delicate, super-valuable freight who could afford to pay for the best. The other way was to load up a rocket and fire it off like a gun, hitting escape velocity in the shortest time with the minimum of fuel. It was cheap, but it was hell on the cargo.

Learhy opened his eyes after the initial blackout and felt as if he had been beaten all over with rubber clubs. Once he had been so beaten, and the sensation was the same. He ran his tongue over his teeth and tasted blood. He tried to move, failed, then remembered the straps. On the third try he managed to unclip himself and drifted from the mattress.

Immediately, he was sick. It was a horrible, retching nausea, which tore at his stomach and made him wish for death. Weakly, clung to the edge of the mattress, fighting the ghastly sensation of falling . . . falling . . . falling . . . which was the result of free fall.

A crewman came down from the

control room. He was a short, stocky man, red-haired and impatient. He wore magnetized boots and walked with the painfully acquired skill of long practice. Learhy lifted his head as the man approached, tried to speak and was sick again. The crewman swore with a savage bitterness.

'Get back on that couch, sludger! You want to foul up the air system?'

'The head.' Learhy made weak gestures. 'Got to go to the head.'

'You ain't going nowhere.' The crewman was strong, stronger in the absence of gravity. He lifted Learhy as if he were a child, clipping him down with a vicious tightening of the straps. 'You stay there till we land.'

'The head.' Learhy could think of nothing else.

'Do what you got to do where you are.' The crewman glowered around the compartment. 'Hear that you sludgers? No one moves for no reason. We touch-down in five hours, then you can clean up the mess.' He walked off, his boots ringing on the floor.

Five hours can be a short time or a long time, depending on circumstances. To Learhy it seemed like eternity. He fought a losing struggle against the straps clipping him to the mattress, the crewman had jerked them too tight and they were cutting off the circulation. Cramps came after a while and he tried yelling for help. None came. He tried appealing to Stanson and Klien, but they were either unconscious or just didn't care. He ended up by cursing the shuttle, the crew and everyone alive in the compartment with prison-filth. Then the deceleration slammed at him and brought welcome black-out.

He recovered to find a crewman unclipping him and heaving him to his feet. He swayed, biting his lips against the pain of returning circulation, then stumbled and fell in the low gravity as the man shoved him towards the entry port.

'Get moving, sludger! The crawler ain't waiting.'

Painfully, Learhy staggered to the port. Other men bumped into him, all of them looking the worse for wear. Two of them carried a limp burden and Learhy recognized Klien. Stanson caught his arm as he moved forward.

'Leave him.'

'But . . .'

'Leave him.' Stanson wiped a smear of blood from his upper lip. 'Too soft,' he said. 'All of us, too soft to take it.'

It was the truth, and none of them had foreseen the danger. Long years in jail don't help a man's muscles, and Klien had lived on the bottle for too long. Compared to the others they were physical weaklings. The forged papers had claimed strength for them, but hadn't been able to give it.

'What do we do?' Learhy kept his voice low, talking prison-wise from the corner of his mouth. 'With Klien out, what do we do?'

'Play it straight.' Stanson led the way into the flexible tube connecting the shuttle to the crawler. 'Play it straight and wait our chance.'

He dabbed again at his bleeding nose.

* * *

Playing it straight meant doing the work they were supposed to do, acting up to the documents which had got them to the Moon. Klien was the lucky one. He rested in the hospital while ruptured blood vessels healed and torn ligaments regained their strength. As a manual worker he was finished, but he was on the Moon under contract to Atomic Disposals and they wanted their pound of flesh. They gave him a job in supply, warned him not to be too generous, then sat back and let him work himself deeper in debt.

'It's hell,' he complained a week after release from hospital. 'I've got to issue the protective clothing to those poor guys and they won't let me do the job straight.'

'You've got it soft.' Stanson looked at his hands, once white and soft, now calloused and black with ingrained dirt. 'You want to get into a suit and start handling those containers for a change.'

'When do we get moving?' Learhy was getting impatient. For weeks now he had sweated with fear and exertion as he transhipped the sludge cans from the power stations on Earth, spilling the radioactive residues into the disposal pits and knowing all the time he was making a gambler's play with death. Theoretically, he was safe. Theoretically, he would come to no harm providing the cans were sealed and providing his suit was cool and that his exposure time was kept below minimum danger level.

But no one could be certain about the cans, not after their trip up from Earth. The spilling machinery was obsolete and required too much manual handling. The suits were too hot and the working time too long. Most of the three-month workers had radiation burns; all of the six-month workers suffered from over-exposure. Learhy wanted to get out and get out fast.

'I'm working on that.' Stanson glanced about the recreation room in which the workers were permitted to spend their off-duty time. A few men hunched over a viewer; they had shared the price of a fifteen-minute film. Another group had gathered around a poker game and a couple of rare ones were wasting time and money writing letters of protest to the newspapers back on Earth.

'How working?' Learhy lit and dragged at a cigarette. He was nervous with impatience; in imagination he could already feel the radiation burns on his skin.

'It takes planning.' Stanson wasn't to be rushed. 'I explained it all once and I don't want to keep on yapping about it. The first step went without a hitch, didn't it?'

'The first step landed us in the next worse thing to jail. Aside from Klien, we'd be better off in the can.'

'You think I've got it easy?' Klien was offended. 'Think again if you think that.' He looked harried and miserable. 'God, what would I give for a drink! I need a drink real bad.'

'Write yourself a ticket for a couple of bottles.' Learhy was contemptuous.

Stanson shook his head. 'Don't blow your top, Learhy. We need Klien. We've got to work as a team; if not, then we're sunk.'

'Am I arguing?' Smoke gushed from Learhy's mouth, but despite his impatience he had to admit that, so far,

27

Stanson's crazy idea had worked out. The first part, at least. To operate the plan they had to get off planet, and he had arranged that. The next part didn't seem so easy.

Waste Disposals was on the Dark Side of the Moon, the side away from Earth. The general landing field was at Tycho Station almost 3,000 miles away. From the Station the big interplanetary ships left for the Tri-Planet runs and all ships with passengers and cargo for Earth had to land there. Tycho was the quarantine station, customs depot and supply point.

'We'll have to wait until we're due for a recreation period,' said Stanson. 'The company runs a shuttle once a month for all those who can afford to pay the return fare. It stays a couple of days at the station picking up mail and flash-stuff for the bosses.' He sucked at his teeth. 'We'll be on that shuttle.'

'We'll need papers,' said Learhy. 'They'll send out an alarm when we don't turn up.' He looked at Klien. 'Can you fix it?'

'No.' The pudgy man looked as if he

were almost ready to cut his throat and so end his misery. 'It takes time to rig papers,' he explained. 'Time and the right equipment. I've no inks, pens, paper, and I can't work without a drink inside of me.' He thrust out his right hand; it was quivering. 'See?'

Stanson's nudge interrupted Learhy's comment. A couple of foremen swaggered through the recreation room, their outside boots tearing at the chipped concrete of the room. They scowled at the three men, seemed about to say something, then moved across to the group around the viewer. One of them deliberately jerked out the cable, cutting short the film. The group dissolved, not wanting to argue about the lost price.

Learhy half-rose. 'Damn screws.' His big hands clenched at his sides. 'I hate screws.'

'Sit on it,' snapped Stanson.

'What are those gimps to you?'

His fingers dug into the other's arm. 'Sit down and listen. We've got to get to Tycho, remember?'

'And that takes money,' chipped in

Klien. 'Cash on the nail.'

That was the least of their worries.

★ ★ ★

Criminals have no ethics, and honour among thieves is a myth. Learhy raised the money by the simple process of robbery, beating up one man who challenged him so badly that he had to go into the hospital. With money to flash they were permitted on the shuttle and arrived at Tycho two days before the terminator was due. The pilot took them through the lock, uttered the customary warning as to what would happen to them if they missed the return trip, and went about his own business. His warning was wasted. They had trouble enough waiting for them back at the workings and didn't intend returning to collect it. But staying in Tycho wasn't all that easy.

The Station had started as a dome and had continued that way. Around and above the original dome others had risen, thin, strong skins of plastic pressurized from within. A big meteor would rupture the skins, but big meteors, those above a few grains, were scarce. Even if they did hit the Station the air-loss would be slight and the minor damage quickly repaired by the AirTechs. The Station was a self-contained unit, which was impossible to enter or leave without permission, and a city like that is a jail. And Tycho was a jail with its own, peculiar laws.

Learhy sat on a hard cot in a room smaller and more bare than the cell in which he had spent five weary years. A cigarette dangled from his lips. It had cost twenty times its price on Earth, part of the extra being the tax for the added oxygen consumption smoking it would entail. A meter-fitted water faucet decorated a wall, a chipped beaker on a shelf above it. He looked up as the door slid open and Klien squeezed into the room.

The forger was cheerful again; the reason was in the bottle he produced from a pocket. He tilted it, smacked his lips, passed it over. Learhy coughed over the raw spirit, the by-product of the yeast vats. 'What is this, rocket fuel?'

'For me it's a lack of depression.' Klien

gestured towards the tap. 'Dilute it if you want. Me, I'll take it as it comes.'

Learhy grunted, took the beaker from the shelf and swore as the tap remained dry. He fumbled in his pocket, thrust in a coin and got five ounces of water in exchange for sixty minutes of manual labour. He cursed as he added liquor to the sterile water. 'Damn slice joint! They've rigged the meter.'

'Survival of the fittest,' said Klien. 'Without papers who are we to argue?'

Learhy's face darkened as he gulped his drink. The underworld extends wherever men congregate, and those who live outside the law can always find somewhere to roost — at a price. He flung the empty beaker against the wall. The plastic shattered and fell to the concrete floor.

'Five days!' he stormed. 'Five stinking days holed up in this coop, paying through the nose for everything we get.'

'It won't last much longer.' Klien was in an alcoholic euphoria. 'Things will break soon.'

'Yeah, they'll break just as soon as we can't pay these harpies to keep us under cover.' Learhy clenched his hands. 'When are we going to move?'

'When Stanson gives the word.'

'When will that be?' Learhy took two strides, turned, took two more and arrived back from where he'd started. 'It's dark outside, isn't it?'

'The terminator hit us three days ago.' Klien tilted the bottle and finished what it contained. 'Doesn't help us much.'

'You check the hotels?'

'As best as I could.' Klien shrugged. 'Not a hope. Those places are sewed up tight with guards. We couldn't even get into the sector.'

'Lousy city! Lousy damn city!' Learhy was burning with impatient rage. Inaction always irritated him, and he had the old, familiar feeling of imminent trouble. It was the criminal instinct, the nervous tension of those who depend on hunches and intuition. Something was wrong and he didn't know what it was. All he knew was that he wanted to get moving and keep moving. He glared at Klien.

'There are tourists walking the domes, aren't there? Flash guys with their dolls?

Easy money if you want it.'

'I've scanned the joint.' Klien refused to be annoyed. 'Tourists and the money crowd are kept behind bars, away from the scum. If they want to go slumming they go covered by guards. With the clothes you're wearing and the way you look you wouldn't get within shouting distance of them. You'd be grabbed.'

'Maybe.' Learhy had his own ideas. 'It could be worked,' he urged. 'If we plan it right we could, maybe, lift a wallet.' He bared his teeth at Klien's expression. 'You getting soft?'

'I don't like violence.'

'You'll get a belly-full when we get kicked out, and maybe reported for the reward. The guards back at the workings will have your hide, and what they leave the men we robbed will finish. You want that?'

'Geeson won't report us.' Klien didn't look as confident as he sounded. 'We paid him well and promised him more. He won't turn us in.'

'Geeson's a rat. He wouldn't hide out his own mother unless she could pay.'

Learhy jerked out the lining of his pocket. 'I'm strapped. No coin. Nothing. You?'

'The same. Stanson took all I had.' Klien looked nervously towards the door. 'Are you sure about Geeson?'

'I don't know.' Learhy hunched his shoulders, fighting the mounting sense of urgency within him. 'I've got a feeling that something's wrong. I had it the last time when the coppers grabbed me, and I've got it now. I . . . ' He broke off at a knock on the door. He jerked open the panel and stared at the girl outside.

She was tall, slender to the point of thinness, her dark eyes huge in the whiteness of her face. Her clothing was cheap and did little for her figure, but she had tried to improve it with a wide belt of gold flexmetal. A second strip of the same material bound her long, blue-black hair. She was one of Geeson's daughters, a courtesy title only, and she was both scared and angry.

'Let me in.' She leaned against the inner side of the panel, her lips red in the light of the glowtube. 'You're in trouble,' she said. 'Bad trouble.'

'Geeson?' Learhy wasted no time. His hard fingers dug into the soft flesh of her shoulder. 'He calling copper?'

'You know?'

'I guessed. Is he?'

'Yes.' She winced and Learhy released his grip. 'I heard him talking to one of the runners. Seems that there's a reward out for you; at least there's one out for three men who broke their contract with Waste Disposals. Geeson wants to collect it.'

'If he turns us in then he'll be in trouble for hiding us.' Klien looked baffled. 'Doesn't he know that?'

'Geeson's got an in with the guards. They make the capture and he splits the reward.' She shrugged, her face cynical. 'It happens all the time.'

'Geeson.' Learhy made a sound deep in his throat. 'Where is he?'

'You going to kill him?' The girl wetted her lips in anticipation. Her eagerness checked Learhy's anger.

'Is that what you want?' His fingers reached for her shoulder again. She twisted away, glaring defiance. 'Well?' He dropped his hand. 'Is it?'

'He took a whip to me.' She bared her teeth at the memory. 'Beat me as if I was a dog. I told him then that I'd get even, and now I am. Kill him, mister. Kill him good.'

'Wait!' Klien was thoughtful. 'What's your name, girl?'

'Lorna.'

'Geeson told me about you. Always making trouble, aren't you? Hard to handle, he said, and said to be careful if you tried anything.' The pudgy man let out his breath in a sigh of relief. 'Relax, Learhy, the girl's trying to needle you into doing her dirty work. Geeson's not going to report us; she just wants you to think he is.'

'Is that the way it is?' Learhy wasn't too surprised; he'd lived in the underworld too long to be shocked or startled at the ways of men and women intent on their own ends. But he didn't like to be used.

'You can think that if you want.' Her contempt was obvious. 'But don't blame anyone but yourself when the guards grab you.' She took a step forward. 'Geeson will flay me if he ever finds out I warned you. Do me a favour, mister. When they grab you, just don't tell anyone that I came here.' She reached for the door, then stiffened as Learhy's hand closed over hers.

'He took a whip to you, you said?'

'That's right.' She looked into his face. 'He beat me, and I can prove it.' Before either man could move she had unzipped her clothing, pulled the thin fabric over her shoulders and bared her back down to the waist. The delicate skin was traced with a criss-cross of angry red lines.

'Still think I'm lying?' She wriggled back into her dress.

'You've been whipped,' said Learhy thickly. 'That's for sure.'

'So she's been beaten.' Klien waved his hand. 'So what? Dames like her are always stepping out of line. But that doesn't mean that Geeson's going to sell us out. It just means that she's mad at him and wants you to get her revenge.'

It was logical, either way it was logical, and, if it hadn't been for his own instinct, Learhy might have accepted Klien's explanation. But he had lived on the thin edge of danger for too long to ignore the signs. He opened the door and jerked his head at Klien.

'We're getting out of here.'

'Why? The girl's lying.'

'Maybe.' Learhy didn't want to argue about it. 'But we're leaving just the same.'

He led the way into the passage, running past the cubicles, heading for the stairs that led to the lower floor. Halfway down he froze, his body stiffening at the sound of voices. Heavy feet echoed from the plastic as men climbed upwards and a figure came into view. It was a thick-set figure wearing the hated uniform of those who upheld the law.

Lorna hadn't been lying.

What happened next happened fast. There was a brief, split second pause of mutual recognition, then, as the guard snatched at the ion gun at his waist, Learhy was on his way downstairs. He didn't walk or run, he simply flung his entire body forward and down, turning himself into a living missile of bone and muscle. The low gravity helped, that and the strength of his legs, but what helped most of all was the speed in which he acted.

The guard touched his gun, drew it, then went down beneath a hundred and eighty pounds of fighting fury. Learhy wasted no time on a second blow; the man was either dead or unconscious, but the guard wouldn't have been alone. He snatched the fallen ion gun, rolled as a blue finger swung towards him, and triggered a bolt at the second guard. His aim was poor, but good enough. The man doubled in uncontrollable muscular spasms as the charge dispersed through his body.

'Back!' Learhy raced up the stairs yelling at the others. 'Up! Get up!'

'Where to?' Klien grabbed at Learhy's arm. 'Where are we going?'

'The girl will tell us.' Learhy knocked aside the hand and reached for Lorna. 'Is there a way out of this warren? The roof, maybe? A window?'

'The roof.' Her long legs gleamed white through the slits in her skirt as she ran upstairs. They passed rows of blank-doored cubicles, each probably containing a human being. No one was curious enough or foolish enough to open a door. Behind them the air began to smell of ozone as the guards, taking time to fire up each flight, came after them.

'Here.' Lorna halted and pointed upwards to where a trap showed in the ceiling. 'That leads to the roof.'

'Good.' Learhy glanced down the last flight, thrust the ion gun into her hand and grabbed at Klien. 'Cover us, girl. You can use a gun?'

'Never had to yet.'

'Point it and pull the trigger at anything that moves.' Learhy heaved Klien's bulk upwards. 'Open it and reach down for us.'

Klien grunted as Learhy almost threw him upwards. His hands and head thudded against the trap. It didn't move, and agonizing seconds passed while he searched for, and found, the lock. It swung back, letting in a gust of cool air and a glimpse of the artificial lights strung on the inner surface of the dome.

'Hurry.' Lorna crouched at the foot of the stairs. 'They're getting closer.'

'Give me the gun.' Learhy took it,

thrust it into his belt, picked up the girl and threw her slender weight towards the trap. He waited until she was through, fixed his legs and flung himself towards the opening. He was almost clear when a bolt touched the calf of his left leg. He rolled, grinning with agony, as Klien slammed shut the trap and sat on it.

'They get you?' Lorna was anxious.

'My leg.' Learhy pounded at the numbed muscles. 'I can't use it.'

'Let me help.' Her fingers were surprisingly deft as they probed at the knotted mass of sinew. 'Better?'

'Good enough.' Learhy tested the limb, wincing at the pain from his semi-paralysed muscles. Klien, safe on the non-conductive plastic, called to him.

'They're getting restless, Learhy. I can't hold them much longer.' He looked worried. 'Where do we go from here?'

'Over the roofs and up onto the higher level.' Learhy gestured towards the thin span of a fly-over. 'Once we get away from the area we stand a chance.'

'With these guards on our tail we won't stand any chance at all.' Klien swore as the trap heaved beneath him. 'Not counting the guards who will be watching around the building.'

'If we move fast we can dodge them.' Learhy scowled down at the trap. Once Klien removed his weight the guards would come boiling out onto the roof. Dodging the cordon guards was just possible; they would take time to get into position, but to dodge the ones below wasn't so easy. It would be impossible unless they could get a start. Learhy stood on the trap.

'Get moving,' he ordered. 'Make for the fly-over; you can jump the gaps and reach it without too much trouble. Move!'

They obeyed the iron in his voice and he stood watching them as they sprang to the roof of the next building. Gun in hand, he tensed, then, deliberately, stepped well away from the trap.

It flung open to a haze of blue, the ion beams lancing in almost every direction.

Luck saved Learhy, that and the fact that one man, no matter how quick or clever, cannot cover three hundred and sixty degrees with any weapon without a time lag. The guard fired blind, then, as he saw Learhy, tried to correct his aim. He never got the chance.

He sagged as Learhy's bolt knocked him unconscious, sagged and fell as the guard supporting him felt the shock of the dispersed charge. In the brief moment before other guards could resume the fire, Learhy sprang forward, jerking back the trigger of his weapon. The opening in the roof became hazed with blue and the stench of ozone wafted to his nostrils. Satisfied, Learhy turned and ran for the edge of the roof, leaping hard from the parapet. He almost missed the opposite roof, his still-numb leg hampering his spring. Desperately, he clawed his way to safety, raced at top speed towards the fly-over and gained it just as the guards opened fire.

'Made it.' Klien sucked at his lips. 'Never saw anyone move so fast in all my life.'

'We've got to keep moving.' Learhy lurched to his feet. 'You know where we'd be safe, girl?'

'Joel's Bar, down by the loading area.

He owes me a favour and he's no friend of Geeson's.' She brushed down her skirt. 'Let's get moving. The guards will turn the Warren inside out after what you've done. They don't like collecting their own medicine.' She glanced at the ion gun in Learhy's hand. 'Better ditch that thing.'

'I'll take care of it.' Learhy tucked it out of sight. Klien glanced back towards the opposite roof and hastily followed Learhy and the girl.

'Stanson,' he said. 'We've got to find Stanson. If he walks back into that mess then we're sunk.'

Learhy didn't answer. He didn't know where Stanson was.

★ ★ ★

Stanson was watching the loading area facing the big, commercial exit ports. The area was brilliant with light from overhead glowtubes and men toiled like ants as they manhandled crated supplies for the ships waiting outside. He wasn't alone. Around him other men waited, casual workers eager for a few hours employment. They were a thin, underfed, scrawny bunch, most with dependents, all without hope. They made good cover.

Stanson waited and watched, and thought about his great idea. The twenty-second century was a time of extremes. The wealthy were impossibly rich, the poor utterly dejected. They had their artificial amusements, but they had no pride. They were serfs in an economic feudal system more rigorous than any previously known. But a strong man, a bold man, could, if he were audacious enough and ruthless enough, break his way free of the system.

Stanson thought that he had found the way.

The ships were the answer; the big, interplanetary vessels which traveled between the worlds. Filled with costly cargo, crammed with pleasure-seeking tourists, they held more wealth than a man could imagine. Stanson wanted that money. He wanted to reach out and take what he wanted so that he could enjoy life to the full. It was risky, yes, but with the right help and the right plan it could be done. He was willing to risk his life on it.

A guard walked towards the waiting men. He halted a few feet from the wire-mesh barrier cutting off the loading area.

'Nothing this shift,' he said. 'No sense in waiting.' He lifted his voice as no one moved. 'You heard me, you guys. Quit cluttering up the fence. Beat it!'

Stanson waited until the others had sulked away, then spoke before the guard could challenge him.

'Just a visitor,' he said quickly. 'Just looking at what makes the wheels turn.' He gestured towards the area. 'Are all the ships loaded from here?'

'Sure.' The guard accepted a cigarette, tucked it in his pocket. 'Where're you working?'

'Air-Tech, start duty next shift.' Stanson hoped his clothes wouldn't betray him. They were shabby but not exceptionally so, and their cut was expensive. He drew at his cigarette. 'Anything due to leave soon?'

'The *Aphrodite* is lifting within the hour.' The guard pointed to where a big

Tri-Planet ship waited on the plain. 'The *Rover III* is taking off after.'

'Is that the one? That small one?'

'Yeah. Charter ship taking a party on a tour.' The contempt in the guard's voice was plain. 'My old man wouldn't have called it that.'

'I get it.' Stanson pointed with his cigarette towards a slender vessel towards the edge of the landing field. 'And that one?'

'The *Armitage*?' The guard shrugged. 'Regular run with fine cargo and top-class passengers. Due out for Mars in about ten hours.' He yawned. 'Wish I was going on her.'

'Nice ship?'

'The best.' The guard yawned again. 'Hell! I'll be glad to hit the sack.'

'A pity.' Stanson jingled some coins in his pocket. 'I was hoping that maybe you and me could dip the bill. Should I call back when you're off duty?'

'Some other time.' The guard looked regretful at the loss of the proffered drink. 'I've five hours to go, and then straight home or catch hell from the old woman.

You know how it is.'

'I can guess.' Stanson shook his head. 'Women are the devil.'

'You said it.' The guard shrugged. 'Had a night of it last night and now I've got to make the peace. You working for Air-Tech, you say?'

'That's right.'

'I'll be looking for you. Me and the boys generally drop in for a snort over at Joel's Bar. See you there maybe?'

'Sure.' Stanson turned away, his face thoughtful. The guards changed shifts in five hours' time; the *Armitage* was due to leave in ten. Close, but it might just be done. Deep in thought, he walked back towards the Warren then jerked to sudden awareness as he turned a corner.

The place was hot. It was so hot it was smoking. Two cop-cars stood in the street and guards were everywhere. Stanson ducked out of sight, his stomach knotted with tension. He jumped and turned, hands half-lifted, as someone touched his elbow.

'You took your time,' said Lorna. She jerked her head and Stanson followed her through a maze of narrow passageways darkened by the fly-overs above. 'Learhy and Klien are safe.' She answered his unspoken question. 'Geeson sold you out. I learned what he was doing and carried the word. I planted your friends and came back to catch you if I could.'

'Do I know you?'

'Lorna, one of Geeson's girls.' She shrugged thin shoulders. 'No more though, not now. You can trust me.'

'Where are the others?' Stanson wasted no time on nonessentials. She had saved him from walking into a trap, and that was good enough to be going on with. He swore as she told him. 'Joel's Bar! That's where the port guards hang out.'

'Joel knows his business,' she said calmly, and laughed at his expression. 'Well, smart guy? You want to come with me or do you want to take your chances?'

Put like that, there was no alternative.

* * *

Joel was a man of indeterminate age, nationality and occupation. His hair was dark, but that could have been dye. His speech was rough, but that could have been camouflage. His clothing was poor, but he resided in a poor area. He ran a small bar, the haunt of dockworkers and port guards, and it seemed to give him profit enough to pay protection and leave a little over.

Appearances are deceptive. Joel could have lived at a tourist hotel and kept servants. He could have lived easy and eaten rich every day of his life. His real occupation, the one that provided all his wealth, while not the oldest, was certainly no youngster. He was a smuggler.

'I've been waiting for you guys.' He drew slowly at an imported cigar. 'Who is the boss-man?'

'Talk to me,' said Stanson quickly. Learhy shrugged, not wanting to argue. Klien, happy with a bottle, beamed around the small room in which they sat.

'I know the background,' said Joel. 'We can skip that. What are your plans for the future?'

'We just want to get along,' said Stanson. 'I was hoping that we could get a berth on a ship.'

'Without union cards, papers or cash?' Joel didn't shrug, but his voice sounded as if he had. 'Three contract-breakers like you wouldn't stand a chance of getting past the barrier.' He inhaled again, savouring the smoke with obvious relish. 'And you can't bribe the guards, either.'

'I wasn't thinking of that.'

'No? For days now you've been hanging around the loading area. You've talked to guards and dockworkers, and, to me, that only adds up to one thing. You want information and you want it bad. If you were legitimate you could get it from the shipping office, but you daren't risk that. So you did it the hard way. The stupid way.'

'Why stupid?' Stanson was always willing to learn.

'The hard way is always the stupid way,' said Joel. 'You made yourself suspicious, and for a man in your position that's stupid.' He brushed a little ash from his cigar. 'You want to ship out?'

'Yes.'

'Any particular place you want to get to?'

'No.' Stanson looked hopeful. 'Can you help us?'

Joel took his time answering. 'Things like that cost money,' he said gently. 'Plenty of money.'

'We'll find it,' promised Stanson.

'How?' Joel let his eyes drift from one to the other. 'Tycho's pretty well sewed up, and the sort of game you have in mind wouldn't pay. Violence isn't necessary to rob the tourists, and it isn't wanted. Try it and there'll be trouble, plenty of trouble.' He busied himself with his cigar. 'We don't want trouble.'

'What you want doesn't worry me,' said Learhy suddenly. He was getting tired of this cross talk. 'If you've a deal in mind let's hear it. If you haven't then stop wasting air.'

'I've a deal,' admitted Joel. He wasn't annoyed. Plain speaking men are usually to be trusted — within limits. 'Lorna told me about you,' he continued. 'From the first I knew who and what you were.' He smiled up at the girl. 'Part of my intelligence service, you might say.'

'Skip the hearts and flowers.' Learhy

was impatient. 'What's the deal?'

'I can get you off the Moon,' said Joel. 'How I manage it is my business. It won't be easy, but it can be done. I've a skipper who owes me a favour, and he'll take you and drop you somewhere. You said it didn't matter where.'

'And in return?'

'One of you is a penman.' Joel glanced at Klien. 'I've some documents I'd like worked on, shipping lists, permits for imports, stuff like that. You fix the papers and I'll fix the passage.'

'You know a lot,' said Learhy tightly. He looked at the girl. 'Your intelligence service?'

'Maybe.' Joel's smile was bland. 'That and loose talk. The alcohol is pretty strong here, do you know?' He got back to business. 'Let's skip the recriminations. Is it a deal?'

'It could be,' said Stanson. 'Klien will work on your papers for,' he glanced at the watch on his wrist, 'for seven hours. At the end of that time you get us on board the *Armitage*.'

'The *Armitage*?' Joel looked blank.

'Why that ship in particular?'

'That's my business. Is it a deal?'

'But you'll be caught, grabbed as stowaways, charged at port of landing.' Joel was baffled. 'Is that what you want?'

'Is it a deal?' Stanson was insistent.

'Sure, if that's the way you want it.' Joel shook his head. 'But I don't get it. What's the point of jumping into trouble?' He looked sharply at Lorna as she drew in her breath with an audible hiss. 'Can you understand it?'

'What does it matter?' Lorna was casual. 'Make the deal and let's get it over.' She followed Learhy as he left the room, Joel already getting out papers and equipment for Klien to start work. 'Learhy!'

'What is it?'

'Joel's a fool,' she said simply. 'He's smart in a lot of things, but he's got a cash-register mind. You know, all profit and loss. If he can't figure the profit, then he can't see the motive.' Her hand rested on his arm, the fingers digging into the flesh. 'Me, I'm different.'

'You're a kid.'

'You grow fast in Tycho. You grow double fast with a man like Geeson. You get appetites too, and sometimes you can see the way to get rid of them.' The fingers dug deeper. 'I'm coming with you, Learhy.'

'You crazy?'

'Sure, as crazy as you are. Crazy enough to see what could happen when three men get working on a ship stuffed with tourists.' She laughed in his face. 'That's the great idea, isn't it? The one Klien talked about when I loosened his tongue. The one thing that is going to . . .'

He moved so fast that she had no chance to avoid his hands. They wrapped around her throat, the thumbs crushing her windpipe. His voice, as he spoke in her ear, was a snarl.

'You talk too much and too loud. Watch your tongue or I'll fix it for good.' He drew her close as a couple of dockhands swaggered from the bar towards the select rooms at the back. One of them laughed as he saw Lorna standing close to Learhy.

'Go ahead, bud. Kiss her, we won't mind.'

'Go to hell,' snapped Learhy, but he kept his face averted, half-buried in the girl's long hair. The long hair that hid the hands wrapped around her throat, the hands, which were ready to kill if she made the slightest effort to attract attention. When the passage was clear he released her, ready to clamp a hand over her mouth if she should scream, ready for anything she might do except the thing she did.

Which was to kiss him full on the lips.

★　★　★

The box was five feet long, three wide and two thick, a coffin-shaped container of flimsy plastawood, indifferently airtight and bound with strong wire. It was supposed to contain bonded supplies. It held Learhy.

It wasn't comfortable in the box. It was impossible to sit upright, lie at full length or do anything other than crouch, knees drawn to chest, head at an angle.

Movement would have helped, but movement would have caused sound and vibration, either of which could betray his existence. All Learhy could do was to curse, and cursing did no good. He had been in the box for hours. He would stay in it until he burst free or someone let him out.

The others were in a similar plight. Stanson could probably stand it well enough; he was small and made of wire. Klien would be suffering; maybe he would faint or find some other escape. Learhy couldn't feel pity for the pudgy man. Loose talkers were dangerous, and Klien had proved himself to be a loose talker. He didn't even like thinking about him. Instead, he thought of the girl.

Strange girl, Lorna, the product of a strange upbringing. She had a different set of morals than the normal girl, the way she had kissed him, for example, after he had almost throttled her. Was it that she admired brute strength? She had hated Geeson for beating her, but it wasn't hard to hate Geeson. Idly, Learhy wondered how she was making out cooped up in her box.

Lorna. He felt again the touch of her lips against his, so soft, so warm, so unexpected. She was thin, but good food would cure that. She knew the world and understood it. She had seen her chance and grabbed at it with both hands. She had guessed the great idea and had wanted a part of it. And they had taken her because they could do nothing else — she had made that plain. If she couldn't join them, then she would ruin them; the threat had been unspoken but it was there. So now she was in a box probably cursing her fate and wishing that she was free of the whole mess.

The box tilted and Learhy forgot the girl. It heaved and swayed, the movement sending stabs of agony through his cramped muscles. He pressed his hands against the sides of the container and took advantage of the external noise to move a little. Only a little, more was impossible. Then he caught the transmitted rumble of wheels and knew that he was on his way.

Supplies from Tycho were loaded

within the domes and run out to the ships on crawler-drawn trolleys. Most of the containers were airtight, or sufficiently so as to make no difference. No difference, that is, if the freight was what it was supposed to be. Canned goods and individually wrapped packages didn't suffer from a brief exposure to low air pressure. But Learhy had no individual wrapping. He heard the thin whine of escaping air and knew that he was in trouble.

The leak was small but difficult to get at. The plastawood container had cracked down one corner, the damage hardly noticeable from within and not noticeable at all from outside. It was minor as damage went, but it was enough to kill the man inside the box. Learhy, wriggling without regard to vibration, tore off his shirt, wadded it, pressed it over the crack.

The hissing continued.

He forced himself to be calm. The leak was small and the box full of air. It should be a simple matter to determine just how long he had; simple, but who can figure out a thing like that? A mathematician,

60

perhaps, but not Learhy, not doubled up in a too-small box and hearing his life hiss away. He pressed the wadded shirt over the crack again, harder this time, but with no more success than before.

The next step was born of desperation. He dug his teeth into the base of his left thumb, biting until he tasted blood. He rubbed the open wound over the crack, smearing the area with blood. The blood was thick, the crack thin. The escaping air forced it deep into the opening, pushing it where it had to go. The expanding air cooled, freezing the blood and filling the crack even more. The hissing stopped.

Learhy, saved from asphyxiation, waited for the next step.

It came when the box was picked up and flung violently down onto something hard. The impact started the leak again, and by the time Learhy had sealed it the violent movements of the container had stopped. It had, he guessed, been transferred from the trolley to the storeroom within the ship. There it had been stacked along with others. There would be no more movement now that the loading was complete. Learhy didn't find anything in that to be grateful for.

The final stacking had upended the box so that he rested on the back of his neck, the full weight of his body above him, his knees scraping the box just before his chest. To turn was impossible; all he could do was to straighten his legs a little. He could do that and wait. Wait until the ship was fully loaded, the cargo compartments sealed and pressurized, the contents checked by the crew and signed for. Wait until the passengers had come aboard, the hub sealed and the ship readied for take-off. Wait until it was safe to move, praying that one of the others would be able to escape, or that not too much weight had been piled on his box.

Wait and wonder how long a man can live suspended upside down with the blood rushing to his head, seeming to fill it like a gigantic balloon so that it swelled and swelled and surely must burst.

Wait until it did burst in a shower of scintillating, transient stars.

★ ★ ★

Learhy gained awareness with a skull that seemed to have been split wide open and a sticky wetness on his left hand. The wetness was from his own blood, surging from the self-inflicted wound. His head, when he examined it, was unbroken. It was only then he realized that he was no longer upside down.

Explanation came as he eased his legs. His box had been racked high in the compartment and because of the ship-spin was now right side up. Briefly he wondered at the lack of acceleration shock during take-off, then remembered that this was a high class ship and the take-off would have been gentle. Not that he would have known about it had it been different. The only important thing was that he was alive.

Barely alive.

His head ached and his eyes felt distended beneath their lids. His lips were cracked and his tongue swollen. He gasped, sweat streaming down his body, stinging where it hit his thumb. He knew that he had to get out of his prison and get out fast. The box was airtight, he had seen to that, and the oxygen was almost gone.

Shoulders bunched, he strained his back against the side of the crate. It was like trying to move a mountain. He gritted his teeth, twisted so that his back was against the other side and tried again. Something seemed to yield a little. Sucking in a lungful of the foul air he tried again, jamming his knees a little higher so as to get better leverage and throwing the full strength of his thigh and back muscles against the plastawood. A wire parted with a spiteful hum, another, then he was falling from the box, his eyes seared by the dim, blue glow of a UV bulb.

He didn't move for a long time after landing on the deck; he couldn't. The pain of returning circulation was bad enough and, coupled with a ghastly nausea, it rendered him helpless. He writhed on the smooth metal, eyes closed, waiting until his tortured muscles would gain life and obedience to his commands. Finally, he heaved himself painfully to his feet and went in search of the others.

'Learhy!' Stanson's smile was a grimace. 'We made it.' He heaved himself slowly from his box. 'The others?'

'Klien's unconscious; Lorna, too.' Learhy ran his tongue over his lips as he stared down at them. 'Klien looks bad.'

'He had less air than the rest of us.' Stanson touched the pudgy man on the throat, feeling for the pulse. 'He's alive.' He crossed to the girl. 'The same. Must have been the cramps that knocked her out.' His voice was little more than a whisper. 'We need water.'

Water was carried in tanks, not in the crated cargo, and access to it was impossible unless they went outside. Learhy settled for some canned peaches, ripping open the crate and smashing the cans against a stanchion. The thick, syrupy juice wasn't water, but it helped. Klien and Lorna recovered while they drank.

'Have some of this.' Learhy handed the girl an opened can. 'Drink slow and easy or you'll bring it all up again.' He handed one of the cans to Klien. 'Slow and easy now.'

'God!' Klien rested his head in his hands. 'I thought I was dying. Now I wish I was dead.'

'Drink some of that juice and you'll feel better.'

'I need a drink,' said Klien. 'Lots of drinks.' He gulped at the thick juice, trickles of it running over his chin. 'Crazy caper,' he muttered. 'Why the hell did I ever get mixed up in it?'

'It's too late for that kind of talk.' Stanson was burning with a feral eagerness. 'We're where we wanted to be, right among the money.' He gestured towards the doors of the compartment. 'Out there is all we want, and it's ours for the taking. A little quick action . . . ' He sucked in his breath, his eyes gleaming at the near-fruition of his great ideal. Lorna was more practical.

'What are you going to do?' Her head jerked towards the doors. 'Out there?'

'Take over.' To Stanson it was simple, he had gone over it a thousand times in imagination. 'We cut down the crew and skin the passengers. Those we can't use we get rid of.' He paced the floor, almost trembling with eagerness. 'We're in a closed cycle, remember. The ship is a self-sufficient unit and it carries plenty of supplies. We can blast her away from the regular flight path, throw her into orbit around the sun, maybe. Once in deep space they'll never be able to find us. We can live like kings, have everything we need. Everything.' He was speaking so fast that his words seemed to blur.

'I'll settle for a drink,' said Klien. 'Learhy, isn't there a drink in this place somewhere?'

'Look for it.' Learhy was curt. 'Get drunk and I'll break your neck. I mean it.' He didn't take his eyes from Stanson. Lorna voiced his question.

'How do we get the loot off the ship?'

'We don't.' In the dim, blue glow, Stanson's eyes shone like polished glass. 'That's the whole beauty of the idea. We don't leave the ship at all.'

⋆　⋆　⋆

Stanson was crazy, there was no other way to account for it. Learhy hunched his shoulders a trifle and his scarred hands clenched. The cargo compartment was small and no place to be cooped up with a crazy man. Stanson noticed the gesture.

'You think I'm off my beam?' He shrugged. 'I got you here, didn't I? I showed you the way to get among the money, right?'

'You got us here,' admitted Learhy. 'I've yet to see it was a good idea.'

'Then you're touched, not me.' Stanson appealed to the girl. 'You've got sense, Lorna, you try and show him. This ship holds everything we need, right?'

'It depends on what you mean,' she said slowly. 'Maybe you'd better tell us.'

'We can work this two ways,' said Stanson quickly. 'We can step out of here, grab what we can and jet away in one of the lifeshuttles. That's the stupid way. With the ship alerted we wouldn't stand a chance. They'd come after us, radio for the Patrol, be on the watch for us at every planet. We'd be lucky to stay alive.'

'We could fix that,' said Learhy grimly.

'Maybe, and then again maybe not. Even if we did fix it we'd still have a small ship and little loot. We'd have to land somewhere and find a fence. We'd be robbed, but we'd expect that. We might wind up with some money in a cool place where we'd be free to spend it. That's the best we can hope for.'

'Sounds good to me.' Klien had found himself a bottle and had regained his euphoria. 'Money, no cops, plenty to drink and an easy life, what more do you want?'

'Nothing, but why go to all that trouble to get it?'

'Because it doesn't get handed to you on a plate,' said Learhy dryly.

'That's just where you're wrong.' Stanson gestured towards the doors. 'Out there is everything we need, everything we can hope for. Money will only enable us to buy what's already laid on. Women? The ship is full of them. Good food? Hell, look at the supplies. Liquor, fine clothes, entertainment, servants, comfort? Name it and it's yours. Not on one crummy planet but here, right next door. Why the hell should we leave it?'

It was a new concept, one Learhy

hadn't thought about before, and it took time to register. Stanson was right, of course; the *Armitage* was a top class luxury vessel catering to the rich tourists. Those tourists, the women at least, would be the most beautiful specimens to be found anywhere in the System. The appointments would equal a palace, the food unrivalled, the entertainment anything they wished.

'We can take the ship off-flight pattern,' said Stanson. 'We can smash the radio and cover the ports. No one need ever know what's happened. To the shipping office it will be just another mystery, the insurance companies will write it off as a dead loss and the Patrol will stop looking. We'll be left, rulers of our own little kingdom, and we'll have everything we can think of.'

'Nice,' said Lorna. 'Real nice.' She looked from one to the other. 'But you've forgotten something. There are only four of us.'

'Numbers don't make that much difference.' Stanson was quick to defend his great idea. 'We can strike hard and strike often. We'll cut down the crew, coop up those we don't kill, starve the passengers into submission.' He made an irritable gesture. 'It can be done, girl, don't think it can't.'

'I could argue that,' she said, 'but I won't. We could probably kill them all at that. But I wasn't talking about that end of it when I said we were only four. I was talking about your end.'

'My end?'

'When you get your little kingdom.' She looked at the men. 'How many women each do you want? Five? Ten? Just a couple? One would be one too many if she has a knife and is unwilling. How many servants? How many chefs? How many men to dance attendance? Everyone you spare will be a knife at your throat, remember that.'

'We can watch it,' said Stanson. 'A couple of us will always be awake and watching.'

'Watching the food being prepared? I could kill any man I had to feed if I wanted to. And how could you watch them all every moment of the time? Klien likes his bottle; a drunkard's not a good watchdog. You probably want your women; how close can a lover watch? Get wise, Stanson, you wouldn't last a week.'

'Shut your mouth!' Stanson was angry at the opposition. 'It can be done if we want to do it. All right, so we cut down to a handful and scare the heart out of them. We hold hostages to make sure they play ball. We break their spirit so that they crawl, begging for the chance to serve us. Don't overestimate the tourists, girl; most of them would be glad to throw in with us if we allowed them to play their games.'

And that was true. The crew wouldn't co-operate; they had their duty. The pampered passengers would; they valued their skins. And in any group there are always those eager to serve in order to gain power. Stanson's idea was crazy, but it could work. And the rewards were high, the highest they could imagine.

'You win,' said Lorna. 'We'll play it your way as far as we can. What now?'

'We get moving.' Stanson looked at Learhy. 'You still got that gun?'

'I've got it.' Learhy produced the

weapon, frowning as he read the charge-indicator set in the butt. 'This won't help much, it's almost exhausted.'

'It will have to do.' Stanson hefted a can of peaches. 'We can use these as missiles or clubs if we have to. The thing is to get out, cut down a few members of the crew and get into their uniforms. Then we head for the control room and take over. From there we can operate the bulkhead doors and split up the ship. The captain will have some guns, and with them we'll have the ship by the tail.' He nodded in satisfaction. 'That's about it. Grab some members of the crew and make for the control room at top speed. Play it safe and easy, but don't waste time and don't be gentle.'

'We're wasting time.' Learhy reached for the door control wheel. He spun it in his big hands and jerked hard.

The door was locked.

*   *   *

The fifth-night ball was in full swing, the lower deck a glittering maze of light and colour as men and women drifted to the music of a selected band. No canned music for the luxury trade of the *Armitage*, no recordings or mass-produced orchestrations. Each piece was unique, heard once and then never heard again, for no human musicians can ever repeat themselves exactly.

Captain Maitland, attending from duty not from inclination, smiled and bowed towards scented women who differed only in degree from the harpies infesting the dives around the spaceports. Men, supercilious because they were the centre of a system designed to make them so, acknowledged the man who guarded their lives with his skill, with a curt nod of the head. Those that acknowledged him at all, that is. Most did not. They couldn't be blamed for that. Maitland was, basically, an employee, and as such was entitled to nothing but the payment for his services.

He turned as his second-in-command trod deftly towards him. Pomeroy retained his half-smile and his salute was something from the book, but his voice, as he spoke quietly in the captain's ear, held a hint of strain.

'Can you get away, sir?'

'Trouble?' Maitland, ever conscious of his responsibility, was quick to ask the important question.

'I don't know, sir. Perhaps it's just something unusual. I thought you should know, sir.'

'Know what?' Maitland was curt. Pomeroy, he knew, envied him his command. 'Wouldn't it be a good idea to get to the point?'

'Yes, sir. I . . . ' Pomeroy broke off as a woman, who was fighting a losing battle with her age, simpered up to the captain. She had a smooth-faced, too-effeminate youngster in tow. Not man enough to give the captain the respect due to his rank, he stared down his nose with an artificial auteur which made Maitland long to kick him where it would do the most good. He resisted the impulse. Should he yield to it, dismissal from the service would be the least part of his punishment.

'Captain!' The woman's voice held a shade less warmth than it would had she been addressing her dog. 'Claude would like to visit the control room. Of course, I know all about your stupid regulations, but I hardly feel that they apply to persons like ourselves. Will you attend to it?'

'Certainly, madam.' By a supreme effort of will Maitland kept the smile on his face. 'Mr. Pomeroy will have the greatest pleasure in conducting the young man. Shall we say at ten tomorrow?'

'Tomorrow?' Painted eyebrows arched. 'Really, captain, you seem to be most uncooperative. I expect you to conduct Claude yourself, immediately.'

Pomeroy may have envied the captain his command, but his own pride in the service drew him to the rescue. He smiled as if he found the old hag the most attractive woman on board and his voice was as warmly intimate as he dared to make it.

'Tomorrow would be best, madam,' he urged. 'At the moment some of the more interesting pieces of equipment are not available for inspection and usage. If you will grant me the honour of conducting your friend tomorrow I can assure you that he will have no cause for complaint.'

'You are most gracious.' Pomeroy was younger than the captain and so had more interest for the woman. 'I have friends, Mr. Pomeroy, and they shall hear of your understanding desire to help.' Her eyes grew hard as she glanced at Maitland. 'So unlike other people.'

'The captain has a great responsibility,' said Pomeroy smoothly. He lowered his voice as he soothed her ruffled feelings, doing his best to exonerate the captain from any intention or desire to offend. His youth rather than his words did the trick. Maitland sighed with relief as he watched the couple move away.

'Thanks, Pomeroy. What was it you wanted to see me about?'

'Two things, sir. Sparks reports an electronic storm lying ahead, and the steward reports strange sounds coming from one of the storerooms.'

'The storm, is it plotted?' Maitland took the important thing first.

'Yes, sir. We should miss it by a comfortable margin.'

'Good. And the noises?'

'Like knocking, or so the steward says.

Permission to open the storeroom, sir?'

'Granted.' Maitland hesitated. It was his duty to investigate the noises, but equally so he wanted to check up on the reported storm. The storm seemed to be the most important. 'Take the steward with you to check on the noises,' he decided. 'Probably some loose cargo; half those labourers at Tycho don't know how to stack a compartment. Let me know what you discover.'

'Yes, sir.' Pomeroy saluted and turned away. The steward was waiting for him just outside the cargo compartment. He recognised the officer and held up a hand, warning for silence.

'Hear it, sir?' He lifted his ear from where it had pressed against the metal. 'Getting fainter now, but still regular. There, hear it now?' The noises had increased. Pomeroy listened to them for a moment, then nodded to the steward.

'Sounds like someone signalling to be let out. Maybe a stowaway. Open up and we'll find out.'

'Stowaway!' The steward shrugged at the impossibility of the idea and spun the locking wheel. Pomeroy handed him the key and he inserted it, twisted, spun the wheel again and pulled. Pomeroy stepped forward as the door swung open, the steward crowding at his side.

Death came before they could recognize the danger.

* * *

'Two of them.' Learhy stared up and down the passage, the ion gun in his hand. 'Only the two of them.'

'We were lucky,' said Lorna listlessly. She leaned against rifled cargo, not looking at the dead men on the floor.

'Water!' Klien's voice was a rasp. 'I've got to have water.'

'We all need water.' Stanson had dragged the bodies into the compartment and was busy stripping them. 'Get into the steward's rig, Klien, you're about his size. I'll take the other.' He glanced towards the door, his fingers fumbling with the zips. 'See anything?'

'No.' Learhy crouched back out of sight should anyone glance down the passage.

Like the others, he looked a mess. His lips and chin were thick with stubble, his skin filthy over the UV induced tan, his hands torn and smeared with his own dried blood. His eyes were bloodshot and reflected his craving for water, a craving induced by five days of drinking nothing but syrup and alcohol. He touched his chin, felt the beard and was reminded of something.

'Get out of that rig, Stanson. With your beard you'd never pass for an officer . . . Give it to Lorna; at least she doesn't need a shave.'

'What about her hair?' Stanson answered his own question. 'She can tuck it under the cap.' He began to strip, cursing the wasted time. 'Here, girl, hurry!'

It was no time for false modesty. Skirt and blouse flew to one side as Lorna donned the uniform. It was a poor fit, but, at a distance, it would pass. She looked distastefully at the blood-stained cap, then pulled it on her head, tucking up her hair.

'How do I look?'

'Fair enough.' Learhy examined her

with one quick glance. 'Bad, but you could be worse.'

'Thanks for nothing.' She stepped towards the door. 'What do I do?'

'Case the passage.' Learhy handed her the gun. 'Look for a cubicle with a faucet. If anyone's inside let them have it. Klien will cover you as best as he can.' He gave the pudgy man a can of peaches. 'Don't worry about smashing them; these cans are stronger than they look.' He glanced down towards the two men on the floor. Both had died from crushed skulls. 'Get moving!'

Lorna was lucky. The third room she examined was a steward's cabin and contained toilet articles as well as a washbasin. Learhy found a jar of depilatory cream, smeared the gooey stuff over his face and waited impatiently for it to dissolve his beard. Klien had run to the tap and was gulping water. Stanson, more nervous than ever, stood guard at the door.

'We should have locked the storeroom,' he said. 'We should have locked it after us.'

'We'll be needing it to dispose of the rest.' Learhy snatched a handful of tissues from a dispenser and wiped the cream and displaced hairs from his face. He tossed the wad of tissue into the chute, pulled Klien away from the faucet and let the stream of water run into his mouth. He felt as if he could drink for ever. He wanted to soak in water, gulp it until his stomach distended like a balloon, replenish every dehydrated tissue at once. He knew better than to try.

Klien lunged forward as Learhy rose from the tap to be short-armed away. Learhy found a beaker, rinsed it, filled it and handed it to the girl.

'Drink slow and easy,' he warned. 'Gulp it too fast and you'll get stomach cramps.' He pushed Klien towards the door. 'Get a drink, Stanson, while Klien watches.'

'We should be moving,' said Stanson. 'We can't afford to waste time.'

'We're not wasting time,' Learhy jerked open the wardrobe and found a couple of uniforms. 'We've got to clean up and get fit, and this is as good a place to do it as any.' He waited until Stanson had taken his drink and then laved his hands and arms. Clean, he donned one of the uniforms and tossed the other to Stanson. In the pockets of his own clothes he found a package of cigarettes, lit one and inhaled with satisfaction. Klien, standing by the door, stared worriedly over his shoulder.

'Someone's coming.'

'Freeze!' The cabin went dark as Learhy hit the switch. He pulled Klien away from the door and crouched by the panel, the gun in his hand. Footsteps echoed from down the passage, seemed to hesitate outside the cabin and then began to fade. Learhy took a chance, cracked the door and peered after the sound. He switched on the lights as he shut the door.

'Two men, engineers by the look of them, probably going off-shift or catching some chow.' He rubbed his forehead, annoyed to find that he was sweating. 'Get washed, Klien.'

'But . . .'

'Get washed!' Learhy leaned back

against the door as the pudgy man hurried to obey. 'When we leave here we'd better go out with a plan,' he said. 'Any ideas, Stanson?'

'I've told you my ideas.' Stanson, now that he had removed his stubble and washed himself, looked a little less desperate then before. 'We head for the control room, fast!'

'Lorna?'

'I'm a passenger.' She hesitated. 'Could we go easy on the killing? Those two poor guys . . . '

'It was them or us.' Learhy had no time for sentiment or squeamishness. 'We haven't got much time,' he reminded. 'That officer was sent to investigate our knocking. When he doesn't report back someone will come after him to see why. We daren't risk the chance of a general alarm, not if we want to stay alive we can't.' He hefted the almost exhausted ion gun. 'Ready?'

'Ready for what?' Klien blinked reddened eyes.

'To do what we came for.' Learhy straightened and drew a deep breath.

'Let's go.' He snapped off the light and opened the door of the cabin.

* ⋆ ⋆ ⋆ *

Captain Maitland was worried. Worry, to him, was no stranger, but this time the keening anxiety was a little more pronounced than usual. The cause, as he knew, was the report of the electronic storm received by the radio operator in a message relayed from the observation satellites scattered throughout space. Knowing the cause didn't obviate the anxiety. If he had been in command of a freighter things would have been easier, but he was in command of a top-class luxury ship with a cargo of passengers who had to be treated with superhuman tact and diplomacy.

'Request a repeat-check on the movement of the storm,' he ordered. 'Top priority.'

'Yes, sir.' The man concentrated on his instruments. 'We won't foul it, sir.' Lambert, the cheerful, cocky navigator, looked up from his computer. 'If the satellites are to be trusted we'll clear it by close on a million miles.'

'Too close.' Maitland was uncomfortably aware of the margin of error in any reported storms. He crossed to the flight chart, a glittering panel of coloured lights traced by a sharp green line. A second line in red reached alongside the green. The green line was their computed flight path, the red their actual course. Lambert had adjusted the panel to show the reported storm, and it sprawled, an untidy mass of black, almost touching the red line. Maitland rested his finger on the chart.

'How soon will we know?'

'Quite a while yet.' Lambert had served under Maitland too long to pay lip-service to discipline. He was loyal, efficient, and probably the only real friend Maitland had. He joined the captain before the panel. 'We could increase speed and make sure of it, sir. The storm is drifting into our line of flight. If we keep to schedule, and if the satellites are to be trusted, we'll miss it. If not . . . ' His shrug was eloquent.

'We hit it and drift until we move out of the affected area.' Maitland had been in an electronic storm before. 'How do you think our passengers will relish the experience?'

'They might find it amusing,' said Lambert dubiously. 'It will be a new experience for them and give them something to boast about.' He caught Maitland's expression. 'Well, perhaps not.'

'They'll scream to high heaven about inefficiency, maladministration and all the rest of it. The company will agree with them.' Maitland didn't have to explain what would happen then. He would be the scapegoat all down the line. He came to a decision. 'We'll accelerate a little. If we do it carefully, say at one-tenth G, they may never notice. We can alter course, too, just enough to swing us clear of the affected area.' He glanced around the control room. 'Pomeroy?'

'Not returned, sir.' Lambert had seated himself at the computer, his fingers dancing over the keys as he set up the problem of course-speed alteration for the master computer to give the firing pattern. 'He's at the ball, I think.'

'He was.' Maitland remembered the incident. 'A steward reported some noises from a cargo compartment and I sent him to investigate.' He frowned at his wristwatch. 'He should have returned by now. Manners!'

'Sir!' a crewman stepped forward.

'Go and find Mr. Pomeroy. You'll find him down in the cargo compartments. He is to report to me immediately.'

'Yes, sir.' Manners saluted and turned away. He wasn't sorry to leave the control room, not when the Old Man was in his present mood, and especially not during the fifth-night ball. He took the long way towards the cargo sector, lingering within range of the music and half-envying the sweating stewards rushing to serve the passengers. They sometimes had to eat dirt, sure, but at least they tasted second-hand luxury, and the tips were good.

Knowledge of Maitland's temper sent him on his way and he walked down the passage between the cargo compart-ments, looking for an open door or signs of the officer. He halted, frowning at the sight of the key thrust within a lock. Keys were retained by the officers. Pomeroy must have used his to open the door. Logic dictated that he must be inside the room. Manners pushed open the heavy metal door.

Sight of the unexpected can sometimes be as great a shock as actual physical violence. Manners had expected to see the familiar sight of racked cargo containers, with perhaps the officer inspecting them. He hadn't expected to see huddled shapes lying on the floor in a puddle of their own blood, and it took a moment for the fact to register. When it did, it was too late.

'Don't move!' The ion gun in Learhy's hand dug into Manners' side. 'Just relax and you won't get hurt.' He thrust the man forward into the room.

'Learhy!' Stanson followed them into the blue-lit darkness. 'Don't waste time.'

'I'm not wasting time.' Learhy didn't take his eyes from the crewman. 'We've got to know what we're doing, Stanson. Running around like a bunch of wild animals will get us nowhere. We can't knock off all the crew and all the passengers, not with just the four of us and an almost empty gun. This character can tell us what we have to know.'

'You..?' Manners couldn't believe what he'd heard. 'You . . . ?'

'We'll ask the questions.' The gun dug deeper into soft flesh. 'Play ball and you won't get hurt, try to act smart and I'll cut you down.' He eased his weight on the weapon. 'Who sent you here?'

'The captain.'

'He expects you back?'

'Yes, but . . . ' Manners winced as the gun dug savagely into his side.

'No questions,' said Learhy mildly. 'Remember?' He frowned in deep concentration. Stanson's plan had failed almost from the start. Without the knowledge of how the ship was laid out, each step they took was a step into potential danger. Already only sheer speed had saved them from discovery, speed and a savage ruthlessness, which had sickened Lorna with its brutality. Bumping into Manners had been sheer luck. Learhy decided to ride it to the limit.

'You're going to guide us to the control room,' he told Manners. 'You're going to show us the way, the safe way, and you're going to act easy and natural and not give the alarm. You do that and you won't get hurt. Understand?'

Manners understood. He had a choice; he could play the hero and die or he could act the coward and live. He wasn't strong enough or intelligent enough to realise that, no matter what he did, his personal end would be the same.

★ ★ ★

It was an uneasy journey. The *Armitage* catered to the luxury trade and so carried a large crew. Normally, they would have been challenged long before they reached the control room; the safeguards to prevent unauthorized intrusion by the passengers would have taken care of that, but things were not normal.

It was the time of the fifth-night ball, the stewards were working double shifts, and what officers could be spared from watch-outs were dancing attendance on the passengers. And Manners was scared. He could have guided them into trouble; instead, he did just what they wanted.

'We're going to get away with it.' Stanson wet his lips as he whispered to Learhy. 'You hear that? We're going to get away with it.'

Learhy didn't bother to answer. He kept close to Manners, the ion gun pressed into his side, the muzzle close to the spine. In such position and at such a range the charge would be lethal. Klien, saddling close so as to give cover, wished that he could have a drink. He had been too long without and felt black depression rising about him. Lorna, trying to walk and act like a man, found time to wonder just how it would all end. Stanson had no doubts.

'Fast and hard,' he whispered. 'Hit them before they know what's happening. Hear that, you others? Fast and hard!'

'Shut up!' Learhy spoke from the corner of his mouth. 'Get ready to act, not talk.'

An officer emerged from the control room, looked surprised as he saw the group, then relaxed as he recognized Manners.

'Did you find Pomeroy?' He jerked his head towards the control room. 'The Old Man's jumping. I . . . '

Klien acted with the fury of desperation. He lunged forward, the can of peaches in his hand swinging towards the officer's skull. There was a dull, soggy sound as the officer crumpled and Klien stared foolishly at the fruit and syrup smearing his hand and arm.

'It broke,' he said wonderingly. 'It broke all to hell.'

Learhy wasn't listening. Even as the pudgy man had acted he had struck once, viciously, at the base of Manners' neck, a hard, killing blow. Even as the officer fell he sprang forward into the control room, the others piling at his heels. Stanson closed and dogged fast the door, and by the time Maitland had turned the room was sealed.

'Freeze!' Learhy gestured with his weapon. 'Move and you collect.'

'What is this?' Maitland, like Manners had been earlier, was numbed by the shock of the unexpected. Lambert was quicker to accept reality.

He rose from his seat at the computer, his hand snatching at a heavy slide rule, his arm swinging back for the throw. Learhy caught the motion and swung, firing at the same time. Lambert doubled, writhing grotesquely on the floor as his muscles jerked to the electrical stimulus. The radio operator joined him as Learhy fired again, the stench of ozone filling the control room. Two other officers went down as Klien and Stanson flung themselves into the attack. Alone, Maitland faced the threat of the ion gun in Learhy's hand. It was exhausted but he couldn't know that.

'Mutiny!' Maitland glanced down towards Lambert. 'Murdering mutineers! You . . .'

'Save it!' Learhy was curt. 'He'll recover if that's what is worrying you. And we're no mutineers.' He stared about the control room. 'Where are the guns?'

'What do you want?'

'The arms locker; where is it?' Learhy

stepped forward as Maitland remained silent. 'Talk, damn you! Talk!'

Maitland wasn't a coward, but he was human, and as such, could experience fear. He experienced it when looking at Learhy. The man didn't need to utter threats; he radiated an aura of desperation. He was a killer, they were all killers, and they would slaughter without compunction. Against such people there was no immediate defence. And Maitland had more than himself to consider.

'There.' He pointed to a small panel set flush in the wall. 'You'll need a key.'

Stanson took the key and opened the panel. Inside rested half a dozen pistols, ion guns, naturally; missile weapons were as suicidal in a spaceship as in a dome colony. The guns were new and fully charged, relics of the time when space madness was a real threat, and only violence could quell physical danger. Armed, some of the tension left Stanson and he began to take command.

'All right,' he said to Maitland. 'This is what you do. First you seal the ship and then you order most of the crew into one of the sectors. Then . . . '

'Slow down.' Learhy checked a pair of ion guns, gave them to Lorna and took the remaining weapon for himself. 'One thing at a time,' he said. 'We seal the sectors, yes, then we talk about what happens afterwards.' He looked at Maitland. 'Show us.'

Maitland hesitated, then led the way towards a panel set with signal lamps and ranked buttons. There was a master button and light at the top of the board. For a moment he toyed with the idea of trying to fool these strangers, then had better sense. Later, perhaps, when their caution had waned from fatigue or overconfidence, but not now. And he didn't know but that one of them might be an ex-spaceman with complete knowledge of the workings of a spaceship. Not that much knowledge was necessary. The panel and instruments were clearly marked.

Stanson looked at the panel, ideas running through his mind. Things had happened fast, almost too fast, and were passing his previously conceived plans.

From now on he would have to improvise. But, as yet, his original scheme could still be worked.

He reached out and pressed the master button.

Lights flared on the panel, winking red one by one and flashing to green as the bulkhead doors slid across passages and corridors. Designed to prevent air loss in case of a ruptured hull or to seal off part of the vessel in emergencies, the doors were both manually and remotely controlled. They could close if the air pressure was below a set limit. They could only be opened if the master panel allowed it, or if the electronic controls were by-passed.

Stanson didn't bother to worry about why they had been installed or how they operated. All he knew was that he had sealed passengers and crew into small, isolated groups. The *Armitage* was now, in effect, a prison, with himself as the warden.

And it would stay a prison just as long as he wished.

★   ★   ★

Nothing succeeds like success, and it is a truism that luck comes to the lucky. Lorna should have felt on top of the world. Instead, she was haunted by a growing doubt.

'I don't like it,' she said to Learhy. 'I don't like it at all.'

'Conscience bothering you?' He didn't ask what it was that she didn't like; he shared her feeling. It was his criminal instinct, perhaps, but he felt that he was sitting on top of an atomic pile with all the dampers pulled out.

She considered his question. 'Maybe. We've gone in pretty deep, haven't we, Learhy?'

'As far as we can go,' he admitted. 'They'll have to dream up something special in the way of punishment if they catch us.' He caught her expression. 'Is that what you're worried about?'

'No,' she said, and he believed her. 'I knew what I was letting myself in for when I joined you. It isn't that, Learhy, it's . . . it's all this.' Her gesture went beyond the control room in which they sat and included the entire vessel. 'It's big, Learhy. It's too big. It scares me.' She wasn't alone in that.

It scared Learhy, too, though he wouldn't admit it, even to himself, and it scared Klien to the point of terror. They had managed to catch a tiger and were holding it fast by the tail — and now they didn't know what to do with it. Stanson's great idea wasn't working as it should. Instead of being kings in their own private little kingdom, they were jailers over a bunch of men and women who were rapidly getting out of control. And, short of mass slaughter, there was nothing they could do about it.

'Stanson scares me,' said Lorna. 'I was with him when we stripped the cabins. There was one old woman still in her bunk . . . ' She swallowed. 'You know what I mean?'

'You're getting soft.' Learhy had no time for weakness. 'It takes guts to get what you want in this world.'

'Maybe I haven't got that kind of guts.' She hesitated. 'Learhy.'

'What is it?'

'Do you believe in insurance?'

'I'm not good at games, girl. If you want to say something, then say it.'

'There's a life-shuttle connected to the control room.' She pointed towards a hatch. 'Down there past a door. You know what I was thinking? I was thinking that maybe it would be a good idea to load it with some of the loot, then, if we have to run for it, we'll have something to show for our trouble.'

'Our trouble?'

'Yours and mine. All of us, what does it matter?' Her fingers closed on his arm and her breath was warm on his face. 'All right, let's face it. I'm thinking of you and me and to hell with the others. Why should we worry about them anyway? Klien's a drunk and Stanson's crazy. Unless we look after ourselves we'll all be caught.' She pressed herself hard against him. 'Well, Learhy?'

She didn't see his face and so couldn't read his expression. He wasn't shocked at her proposal, but he didn't like it, either. Learhy had few ethics and no moral compunctions, but he had learned the hard way that the only way to survive is to unite. Once they let their partnership be broken, they would all wind up as compulsory subjects for vivisection without the benefit of anesthetics. The time for self-seeking and double-crossing might come later, but not now, and not while they each needed the other.

'Well, Learhy?' she said again. 'Is it a deal?'

'Maybe.' He pretended to think about it. 'Tell you what. You load the life-shuttle with the pick of the loot and make sure that there is plenty of food, air and water.'

'Then it's a deal?'

He smiled into her face. 'Sure, why not? But there's no need to rush things. We've got the chance of a lifetime here to make our pile, and we don't want to leave anything behind. You do as I say and wait for the word.'

'And Stanson?'

'I'll worry about Stanson.' He rose as the ship phone buzzed. 'That must be him now. I'll handle it.'

Stanson was irritable at being kept waiting. Klien, smiling foolishly, was at his side. They entered the control room and Learhy dogged fast the door behind them. Stanson glowered at the heaped boxes on the smooth floor.

'What's all this junk doing in here?'

'I like it,' said Lorna. She was defiant. 'Money, jewels, fine clothes, what more could a girl want?'

'I could tell you,' hinted Klien. He winked and burped. 'If I was younger, I could show you, too.'

'Save it for later.' Learhy didn't look at the pudgy man. 'Well, Stanson, any more brilliant ideas?'

'We took the ship, didn't we?' Stanson fumbled a cigarette into his mouth, puffed it to life and almost immediately threw it aside. 'Maybe it's your turn to do some thinking.'

'I've done it.' Learhy helped himself to a drink from the bottle in Klien's pocket. 'So far we've taken over the ship, locked the officers in a cabin, sealed off the engineers and other crew in various sections of the vessel and cooped all the passengers up in the lower deck. We've also stripped the cabins of everything of portable value, cracked open the Purser's safe and smashed the radio. Now what?'

'Hostages,' said Stanson.

'More loot,' said Klien. He tilted his bottle. 'They were having themselves a ball when we took over,' he explained. 'The passengers must be loaded with portables in the way of gems and wallets. What say we collect?'

'Hostages,' said Stanson again. He ignored the pudgy man. 'We threaten to cut down say, twenty passengers unless the officers play the way we say. If they don't agree, then we double the original figure.'

'And when we run out of passengers?' Learhy was ironic.

'We won't.' Stanson knew what he was talking about. 'Those monkeys believe in a thing called duty. Their first duty is to the welfare of the passengers. They won't argue when we tell them what we want done and what we'll do unless it is done.'

'Why don't we just cut and run for it?' said Learhy suddenly. 'We can take what we've got and live easy on the Asteroids.'

'No.' Stanson was determined. 'We'll

play it my way.' He bared his teeth in sudden anger. 'Those monkeys will jump when I give the word or they'll suffer. They'll fall in line when they see we mean business.'

Learhy didn't comment, he wasn't so sure.

* * *

The cabin was small, stuffy, filled with foul air and the effects of too many men compressed in too small a space. Maitland, his uniform creased and rumpled, sat in one corner, his back against the wall. Around him the other officers sat or lounged as best as they could. The only light came from a UV store-bulb. There was no water.

'How long?' Lambert had recovered from the effects of the ion bolt and, aside from an unusual pallor, showed no apparent ill effects. Others were not so fortunate.

'How long what?' Maitland guessed that the navigator was trying to make conversation. 'How long can we live without fresh water or fresh air? How long we've been cooped up in here? How long those pirates can hold the ship? What do you mean?'

'Take your pick,' said Lambert. 'How did they get on board in the first place?'

'Hidden in the stores.' Maitland glowered at the dim bulb. 'But that isn't important. What is important is that they have the whip-hand.' He gave a sound between a snort and a laugh. 'Four people, one of them a woman, and they get away with a thing like this. Pomeroy dead, Manners, a dozen others. Who would believe it possible?'

'It's happening.' Lambert winced as he moved, his muscles still sore from the effects of the ion bolt. 'The question is, what happens next?'

'We'll win in the end,' said Maitland. 'We have to win. They need us to service the ship, tend to the air and engines. Once we get out of this cage . . . ' His voice trailed away in visions of beautiful vengeance. Not that it would do him any personal good. As the captain he was responsible for what happened on and to his ship, and he was effectively ruined. No Board of Inquiry would accept the excuses he had to offer, and they would be right. But that was small consolation.

Time passed and the air grew thicker, their thirst more demanding. None of them had a watch. Stanson had seen to that. Both he and Learhy knew from experience the uses to which the most innocent mechanisms could be put by determined prisoners, and had taken no chances. They hadn't stopped to think, or hadn't bothered to worry about the effects of stale air and no water on wounded men. Maitland was glad when the noisiest of them, a man with a splintered skull, lapsed into unconsciousness. His moans had been affecting them all.

'Someone's coming.' Lambert, resting with his back against the door, had felt the vibration of the turning wheel. 'Do we rush them?'

The door swung open before the captain could answer, and brilliant light streamed into the cabin. Stanson, a gun in each hand, gestured for Maitland to step outside.

'Only the captain,' he warned. 'The rest of you try anything and I'll stop his clock.'

'What do you want?' Maitland blinked in the bright lights of the passage. Learhy, as alert and cautious as ever, stood behind one side of Stanson. Lorna, together with Klien, stood well out of range of any possible rush. Lambert's suggestion would have proved futile.

'We've come to make a deal,' said Stanson. 'You agree to operate the ship and do as we say and no one gets hurt.'

'And the alternative?'

'Twenty passengers get shoved out of the airlock.' Stanson moved closer and lowered his voice. 'Play it smart, captain, what have you to lose? Ride along with us and we'll cut you in for an equal share. Go against us and you'll be responsible for the deaths of your passengers.' He stepped back. 'The choice is yours.'

It was, as he knew, no choice at all. Maitland had to think of the welfare of both passengers and crew, as well as his ship. If he had to agree to help Stanson in order to do that, then he had to agree.

Not for one moment did he delude himself into thinking that Stanson was trying a bluff; the man had gone too far for that.

'I'll need my officers,' said Maitland. 'I can't run the ship without them.'

'Then you agree?' Stanson was jubilant, Learhy was not. He knew that Maitland was only waiting for an opportunity to strike back.

'How many officers?' said Learhy.

'At least a third. My navigator, radio operator, chief engineer . . . '

'You can have your third.' Stanson was impatient. 'The rest we keep as hostages. Try anything and they get theirs together with the passengers.' He gestured towards the cabin. 'Call out those you need.'

'Learhy.' Lorna had moved closer while Stanson had talked to Maitland. 'This is wrong, Learhy, you know that. Once let them birds out of their cage and we're in trouble. Stanson trusts them, I don't.' She kept her voice low. 'That insurance I spoke about; it's fixed and ready.'

Learhy nodded, feeling the old, familiar tension in his stomach. Something was wrong and he didn't know what. His instincts screamed incipient danger at the same time that his logic told him that there could be no danger at all. They were armed, the officers were not. They were in favourable positions while the officers were blinking in the relatively harsh glare of the passage lights. If they tried anything they could be cut down under a hail of ion bolts.

He was still worrying about it when the lights went out.

There was a split-second of silence and immobility, then a furious rush of bodies. Learhy jumped away from where he'd been standing, jerking the trigger of the ion gun, which refused to fire. Something banged into him and a heavy object smashed across his nose. Maddened with pain and rage, he struck out with the pistol, feeling the jar of the blow run up his arm. In the darkness, Stanson was cursing with a frenzied violence.

'Kill them! Cut them down! Don't let them get away!'

'Shut up, you fool!' Learhy kicked and elbowed someone who clawed at him.

'Klein! Lorna! To me!'

If they heard him they didn't answer. Blinded by the sudden dark, they were in a worse state than the officers who had come rushing from the cabin. Grunts and cursing interspersed with blows and the echoes of racing feet echoed from the walls of the passage. Then harsh brilliance was all about them as the lights flashed into life.

'Learhy! Klien!' Stanson spun, his guns eager for targets. 'What happened?'

'Someone gimmicked the lights.' Learhy wiped blood from his face. 'They get away?'

'Gimmicked the lights? How?' Stanson was baffled.

It was a stupid question and Learhy didn't waste time answering it. He dropped to his knees beside the slender figure half covered by the bulk of a man. The man was breathing with difficulty, Lorna wasn't breathing at all.

'Lorna!' Stanson stared down at her. 'Hurt?'

'Dead.' Learhy touched the thick hair, matted now with blood, remembering his own, violent blow. His fault? One of the officers? Stanson, perhaps, or Klein? Not that it mattered; in the dark anything could have happened. She was dead and this was no time for mourning.

'Learhy!' Klien heaved himself to his feet, holding the pit of his stomach. He was ashen pale and had lost his gun. 'Someone kicked me.' He saw Lorna. 'Dead?'

'They took their chance,' said Learhy. He glanced at the lights, burning steadily as if nothing had happened. 'Now they've got away. Let's get out of here.'

He led the way to the control room, knowing that it was too late. He skidded to a halt as the blue finger of an ion gun reached towards him, ducking just in time. Desperately, he raced away from the control room, the others at his heels.

'The passengers!' Stanson was clutching at straws. 'We've still got a chance.'

'No chance at all.' Learhy paused before a panel, his fingers tearing at the fastenings. 'Maitland's back in control. He'll open the doors and release the passengers and crew. We could get some of them, but not all.' The panel swung open. 'This leads to the life-shuttle, a second route to the one from the control room. If we move fast we may make it.'

Stanson took the lead, running down the narrow passage at top speed, his eyes glaring like those of a trapped animal. Learhy came next, followed by Klien. The pudgy man was hurt. Whoever had kicked him had known their business, and he sweated with agony as he tried to keep up with the others. Even Learhy's warning couldn't spur him on.

'Maitland may pull the same trick we did. If he shuts the doors before we reach the shuttle we're sunk.'

'Can he do that?' Stanson kept his eyes ahead and alert for danger.

'He can.' Learhy didn't bother to explain how he'd examined the life-shuttle installation in company with Lorna. 'And if he's as clever as I think he is, he will. He knows this ship better than we do, remember.'

Klien groaned as the others drew away. His legs felt like lead and the pain from his groin was worse than anything he'd ever imagined possible. He wanted to drop, to curl into a ball, to hide himself away from the world with his misery. Instead, he forced his legs to carry him closer and closer to safety. He was almost up to Learhy when it happened.

'The door!' Stanson screamed the warning. 'He's beaten us to it!'

Just ahead of them a thick door was falling from the ceiling. It didn't drop as it would have done under emergency operation, but it was wasting no time. Stanson wasted none, either. He flung himself forward and down, literally diving under the panel. Learhy did the same, feeling cold terror as he clawed his way to safety. Klien wasn't so lucky.

He screamed as he felt the lower edge of the panel bite into the small of his back. He kept screaming as it dug deeper. Stanson paid no attention; he was too busy ripping open the life-shuttle. Learhy hesitated, saw that there was nothing he could do, and followed Stanson into the tiny ship. The door had no emotions, either, it just kept closing.

'Close!' Stanson wiped sweat from his face. 'How do we operate this thing?' His hands were moving even as he spoke, pressing the priming buttons, tripping the release, twitching as they waited for the external plates to move out of the way. Learhy, having sealed them in, took the co-pilot's chair.

'Can Maitland stop us now?' Stanson was a bundle of nerves. 'Damn monkey! Gimmicking the lights the way he did. We . . . ' He grunted as stars suddenly shone on the viewplate. 'Here we go!'

Like a flung stone, the tiny shuttle darted from the flank of the *Armitage*, the release gear sending a rapidly dissipating cloud of vapour after them. Safely clear, the rockets flared into life, thrusting the little vessel into the immensity of space.

Thrusting it directly towards the heart of the electronic storm.

* * *

Stanson spun the ship, building up the centrifugal force to simulate just under half Earth's gravity. That done, he concentrated on where they should go.

'Mars?' He turned and looked at

Learhy. 'Shall we make for Mars?'

'The *Armitage* will be there before us.' Learhy stared at the dwindling image of the ship on the afterplate. 'They're on the economical orbit, and we haven't the fuel to try any tricks.' He frowned at the after-image, then concentrated on the foreplate, brilliant with its array of stars. The coleostat compensated for the ship-spin and the clarified electronic picture showed a host of glittering points.

'The Asteroids, then?' Stanson was undecided. 'You figure we could get that far?'

It was talking for the sake of making noise, and both knew it. In space a ship kept moving until something stopped it, and the only limiting factors to any journey were food, water, air and time. They had plenty of time.

'How about Ceres?' said Stanson. 'I've heard tales about Ceres. Or maybe we should try to make Zelgan. You fancy Zelgan, Learhy?'

'One or the other.' Learhy wasn't interested. Stanson glared his impatience.

'We're in this together,' he reminded.

'It's your neck, too, don't forget. Snap out of it and take an interest. What shall we do?'

'Head for the Belt.' Learhy stared coldly at his companion. 'Neither of us is a navigator and couldn't hit where we wanted, anyway. Just concentrate on reaching the Asteroids and we'll take it from there.' He snorted as Stanson jabbed ineffectually at the controls. 'Use your head, man. Take a sight on the *Armitage* and head in the direction they are going. We busted their radio so they can't send word ahead, and once we cut our jets they won't be able to spot us, either.' He returned his attention to the screen.

Stanson muttered to himself as he took the sight and spun the gyros to align the vessel. He was no pilot and, though every instrument was clearly marked for amateur operation, he felt out of his element and unsure of himself. Savagely, he jabbed his thumb against the firing button. Learhy, silent in his chair, took no notice of Stanson's bad temper.

He was thinking and felt depressed.

Behind them the *Armitage* dwindled out of sight, lost among the glittering stars. Before him the universe seemed empty of familiar life. It was probably the reaction from strain, the letting down of tension, he didn't know, or care. All he could think of was a girl lying silent with blood-matted hair and a man who had screamed beneath the thrust of a closing door. Neither memory was pleasant.

Stanson had left the control chair and was prowling about the cabin. He halted by the side of a heap of boxes, tugging at the lid of the topmost. He cursed as he saw what was inside.

'Loot! The stuff we took from the ship. Learhy, you know about this?'

'Lorna stacked it.' Learhy didn't look from the screen.

'Lorna!' Stanson said something vile. 'So she was getting ready to run out on us, was she? That . . . '

'It was insurance.' Learhy quelled a rising anger. 'She guessed that things might get out of hand and didn't want to leave everything behind. I knew about it.'

'I didn't.' Stanson slammed the lid of

117

the box. 'I should have been told.' He chuckled at a sudden thought. 'Not that I'm arguing, not as things turned out. There's more than enough here to set us both up for life. Both of us, Learhy, you hear that?'

'Sure.' Somehow Learhy couldn't thrill to the thought of the wealth they carried with them. Later, perhaps, but not now. Stanson felt differently about it. He couldn't stop talking about what they carried, what they would do when they cashed in, how he would live, the tricks he would pull. Like Learhy, he was suffering from reaction, but his reaction took a different form. Failure had been turned into success and it went to his head like wine.

Learhy heard the voice without hearing the words. He sat and stared at the viewplate, feeling nothing, wanting nothing, at rest for one of the few times in his entire life. His vision blurred a little from fatigue and the stars wore tiny haloes, shimmering rings caused by tiredness. Pretty little rings, so small, so delicate, so . . .

The stars went out. The signal lamps on the instrument panel died. The drone of the rockets died. The cabin lights died. Everything in or about the ship died save its momentum.

And the two men who sat in sudden darkness.

★   ★   ★

It was total, that darkness, as if the very sight had left their eyes and, for the moment, that is what Learhy feared. Then he heard Stanson fumbling towards the panel, his hands scrabbling over switches and buttons. 'Dead.' Stanson tried again, the switches making dry clicking sounds. 'Everything's dead. I don't understand it.' He stood helpless and a little afraid in the thick, cloying darkness.

'I do.' Learhy had a sudden memory. 'Remember when the lights went out back in the ship? The time the officers rushed us and the ion guns wouldn't work? At the time I thought that someone had gimmicked the lights, but I was wrong. They couldn't have gimmicked the guns, too, and they worked before and after the light failure.'

'So?'

'So it was something outside the ship which caused it, not something inside. The only thing it could be is a solar storm. We must have just brushed it in the *Armitage*, but when we took off in the shuttle we headed straight towards it.' Learhy gave a dry laugh. 'Think of it, Stanson. Of all the directions we could have taken, we had to take the wrong one. Funny, isn't it?'

It wasn't, and they both knew it. Space was a vacuum only in the material sense. Great areas of electromagnetic disturbance — caused by solar eruptions — drifted between the planets and within such an area every man-made electronic device ceased to function. The crew of any ship caught in a storm could only sit and wait and hope they coasted clear before their supplies ran out.

'Light,' said Stanson. 'We've got to have light.' His breathing sounded harsh and strained as he fumbled at the useless controls. Learhy remained calm. He found a cigarette, puffed it to life and held it towards Stanson while he lit another.

'Take this,' he ordered. 'Keep it in your mouth. That way we'll both know where the other is.'

'You think we can see by the light of a couple of cigarettes?' Stanson was irritable. 'Hell, they just give a glow. What we need is something to burn.'

'These are better than nothing.' Learhy puffed his cigarette to brighter life, the ruby tip throwing his face into harsh relief. 'There should be a survival kit in here, somewhere. Let's find it.'

★   ★   ★

They found it after an eternity of groping in darkness, aggravated rather than relieved by the twin spots of red from their cigarettes. It contained some assorted junk, electronic for the most part and so useless. It also contained a sealed box of archaic matches and three candles, testimony of the failure of science when confronted with the fury of an electronic storm.

Fire spurted as Stanson struck a match and a halo of light grew around the wick of a candle. Carefully, he stood it on the instrument panel, cursing as it toppled over extinguishing the flame. He re-lit it, and learning from experience, fastened it with a blob of wax.

'That's better.' Light restored courage and banished the bogies of the dark. 'Much better.' Stanson rubbed his hands, pleased with his success. 'Any chow in this crate?'

They ate from cans, gulping hot, sweet coffee and steaming, savoury stew from containers, heated by built-in chemical units, then relaxed, smoking in the soft light of the candle. It was a machine-made candle, neat and precision-hard. It burned with a steady, unwavering glow, the light dancing from the blank metal of the cabin, the blank expanse of the viewplates. The light, the food, the relaxation made them drowsy and they dozed a little. The candle burned out in a guttering flame amid a pool of wax, flaring a little before it died.

Stanson lit the second candle.

'How long?' he said when he returned to his seat. 'How long before we coast out of the storm?'

'Depends on how big it is,' said Learhy. 'The direction it's drifting, a lot of things.'

'I know, but how long do you figure?' In the candlelight, Stanson's eyes looked furtive. 'Days? Weeks?'

'Worried?' Learhy blew smoke towards the candle and crushed out the butt of his cigarette. 'I can't answer that. All we can do is wait.'

So they waited while the second candle burned into the past. Learhy must have slept a little, a tormented sleep filled with distorted visions of a dark-haired girl and a screaming man. Once he jerked into awareness to find Stanson lighting the third candle. He awoke again when it was almost gone, to find Stanson stooped over him, a peculiar expression on his face.

'Trouble?' Learhy was instantly alert. The pounding of his heart and the taste in his mouth gave the answer. 'Air bad?'

'This crate's on a closed-cycle system,' said Stanson bitterly. 'While the machines work it's just fine, but when they don't . . . ' His gesture was expressive. The shuttle worked on re-using the stale air, cleaning, filtering and re-oxygenating it by forced draught through sealed tanks of algae. As a system it was foolproof and almost everlasting — while there was electric power to keep it operating.

Learhy sat upright, adjusting his personal equations. Nothing had really altered; there was nothing either of them could do but wait until they had passed out of the area of the storm, but the fouling of the air added a time limit. They would pass out of the storm eventually, but they might both be dead when it happened.

But there was nothing they could do but wait.

The third and last candle died and darkness closed around them. In the darkness Learhy heard Stanson fumbling at crates and boxes, then a match flared to reveal him holding a can.

'Wrong one!' He cursed, threw it

down, grabbed another. 'Got it!' He tossed the matches towards Learhy. 'Give me a light to work by.'

'What are you doing?' Learhy was curious. He lit a succession of matches as Stanson tore open the can and freed the mass of thick, greasy paste it contained.

'Making a candle.' Stanson glared around the cabin. 'We need a wick, something absorbent to soak up the grease.' Medicines and drugs spilled from the medicine cabinet as he ripped it open and foraged inside. He ripped open a packet of gauze, twisted it into a thick strand and began to shape the vitapaste around it. The can had been a seven-pound container, it made a big candle.

'This should do it.' Stanson set it upright on the remains of the machine-made products and lit the shapeless wick. It spluttered, smouldered and went out. He tried again, using the heat of the last match to melt a little pool of grease at the base of the wick. This time it burned, badly, unsteadily, but it burned.

'That'll do it.' Stanson stepped back,

well away from the candle. 'It'll last as long as the air does, if no one blows it out.' He ran his tongue over his lips. 'Any idea how long, Learhy?'

'Until we clear the storm?' Learhy shrugged. 'No.'

'It might be days,' said Stanson. 'Or it might be hours. It might be just after the air gives out and we're both dead.' He lifted his hand as if to scratch the back of his neck. 'Or . . . '

With any other man it would have worked, but not with Learhy. He could add and divide as well as Stanson, and he was just as amoral. How long the air would last he didn't know, but one thing was sure — it would last one man just twice as long as it would last two.

And he had seen other cons who carried a knife tucked behind their collar.

Even at that it was close. Steel burned his side as he twisted from its path and his hands, hard and strong, almost failed him as he grabbed for knife-wrist and throat. Then the knife fell from numbed fingers and Stanson stared from a congested face, eyes popping, mouth open for the air he couldn't suck into his lungs.

He was dead when Learhy finally released him. He had strained upwards towards the last, flinging himself against the light gravity and, when released, he hovered for a moment towards the region of null-G along the axis of the ship. Then Learhy pulled him down and sat him on the floor against the boxes so that he could stare at the candle he had made. Against the boxes which held the looted wealth of the *Armitage*, the fruit of the great idea. Down on the floor where the air was too thick and stale for living lungs.

Down in the dirt where he belonged.

★　★　★

The tiny flame flickered, ebbing and almost quenched by rushing shadows before it rose again; a soldier of light battling against the relentless dark. Learhy tensed in automatic reflex then relaxed as the flame steadied. The flame still burned, he could still breathe. The light still shone, he could still see. And

127

while he breathed and could see, he was alive. He could feel and hope and remember. He could think and let the haloed flame dim his vision as it danced and swayed on its sagging column of grey. A tiny flicker of gold surrounded by masses of dark. Darkness so like the strands of a woman's hair . . .

A strange girl, Lorna, a product of the Luna slums, hard and ruthless, ready and willing to take what she wanted, and pay the price if she had to. But hard and clever as she was, she hadn't realised that in any gamble there was only one real winner, and that in the gamble of life that winner was fore-ordained.

Klien, too; he had taken his chances, and, like the girl, like Stanson, he had lost as he had to lose. As Learhy himself had to lose in the long run. As all men had to lose. For in the gamble of life death is the only winner.

But death can be cheated for a short time, and, men being what they are, Learhy still hoped that the air would last, that the candle would burn until the ship coasted free of the storm and life returned to the dead thing of metal and plastic, wires and instruments. The air would flow then and there would be light and humming power and the entire System to rove in.

If the air lasted out.

If the candle continued to burn.

So he sat and watched and died a little more each time the flame died, and lived a little less each time it rose to beat back the dark. He sat and waited because there was nothing else he could do, sat and felt himself going slowly insane to the pulse of the flame . . .

. . . As it died

. . . As it rose.

. . . As it died.

Waiting . . . waiting . . . waiting . . .

Not even knowing how to pray.

Asteroid mining will be a hazardous as well as a monotonous job when ships eventually reach out to the Belt to extract the mineral wealth lying there. The hazards will not all come from rocks in their orbits either.

FORGETFULNESS

Redfern was the one who found it. Big, slow, good-natured Redfern with his easy smile and vivid imagination. He stared at the spectroscope and his yell jerked Murry from where he lay in uneasy slumber.

'Hey! Murry! Look what I've found!'

Murry grunted and, swinging his legs over the edge of his bunk, drifted from the tiny sleeping cabin into the passage leading to the control room. 'Found what?'

'It! The thing we've been looking for!' The big man stabbed his thumb towards the tell-tale lines on the plate. 'See?'

'Wait a minute.' Murry rubbed at his eyes, and stooped a little closer to the spectroscope. The pattern of bright and dark lines faded even as he watched and he swore with the easy fluency of a man to whom cursing was second nature. 'It's dead.'

'I'll liven it up again.' Redfern swung the butt of the thermite gun into the hollow of his shoulder, peered through the sights at something far out in space, and squeezed the trigger. The cough of the weapon was almost immediately followed by the reappearance of the spectroscopic pattern as the burning thermite vapourised the surface on which it rested. 'Now do you see it?'

'I see something,' grunted Murry, his little eyes narrowing as he read the lines. 'Iron, carbon, some copper . . . '

'Platinum and,' Redfern's finger touched the screen, 'Osmium. Osmium, Murry! The heaviest substance known!'

'Yeah.' Murry straightened, one leg automatically hooking itself around a stanchion to prevent him drifting away. 'How big is it?'

'It's big, Murry. Almost too damn big to be true!' Redfern stared at the fading lines on the spectroscope. 'Think we can handle it?'

Murry shrugged. He was smaller than Redfern, much smaller, with a kind of uneasy restlessness, which revealed itself in a constant flickering of the eyes and a subconscious jerking of the head. Compared to the big man he was a midget but what he lacked in animal strength he made up in animal cunning. Now he stood, his slight body swaying a little from the reaction of his movements, his little eyes heavy with thought.

'We could mark it and take the co-ordinates,' he said, more to himself than to the big man. 'Then we could register the claim and sell out to a combine. We could do that and maybe get a twentieth of its value — if we didn't get swindled out of our claim and if claim jumpers haven't found it after we'd left.'

'That don't sound so good,' protested Redfern. 'Why can't we get it all?'

'Or we could mine it here and now, take as much as we can and trust to luck that no one finds it again after we leave.'

'Why can't we mark it and register the claim?' Redfern stared through a port towards the dim shape of the rich asteroid. 'Then we can come back either alone or with a combine to take out the osmium.'

'If we mark it the radio-beacon will let every claim-jumper in the Belt know that we've made a strike and they'll be swarming here to shift markers and fill their holds before we could touch down on Mars.' Murry shook his head. 'That ain't the wise thing to do, Red. Not unless we can stay here to protect our find and we can't do that.'

'They'd respect the markers, wouldn't they?' Redfern stared at Murry. 'I thought that the Belt had been cleaned up years ago?'

'If you thought that then you've got a lot to learn.' Murry grinned as if at a pleasant memory. 'Who's to worry about a couple of bum prospectors and a junky old ship? The Patrol? Hell! They'd never be able to prove a thing even if they could police the Belt, which they can't. The buyers? All they care about is getting valuable ore cheap. Our so-called friends? They'd be the first to pick up our signal and blast in for the kill. No, Red, you've got to be smart to get rich in the Belt, and you've got to be smarter if you hope to live to spend it.'

He sucked at his teeth and something like a smile twisted his lips at the other's expression of incredulity.

'You think I'm joking? Listen, Red, I've prospected the Belt for twenty years now and I know what I'm talking about. That thing,' he jerked his thumb towards the port, 'can either set us up or put us down. It all depends on how we handle it.'

'We could radio the co-ordinates to Mars,' suggested Redfern. 'Wouldn't that authenticate our claim?'

'Sure, unless some tout intercepted the message, or a dishonest clerk saw the chance to make an easy piece of change.' Murry shrugged. 'On a small strike it wouldn't matter, the combines can afford to let the small fry alone, but you said that this one was big.'

'It is big.'

'How big?' Murry gestured towards the instrument panel. 'Give me facts, figures, some dope I can chew over. Hurry!'

Redfern flushed a little at the other's tone then, his easy nature asserting itself, he turned towards the panel.

He was younger than Murry, younger in years and a baby in experience. Fresh out from Earth with a few degrees after his name and some cash in his pocket he had been lured by the glittering prospect of an easy strike. The Asteroid Belt was littered with the corpses of those who had imagined the broken shards of some planetary explosion to be plums ripe for the picking. The wealth was there, yes, but death was there too. Death from the unpredictable orbits of the tiny worlds, from the massive giants of several tons to the tiny ones of a few ounces. Both could kill. The big ones by sheer weight and momentum, the small ones by their bullet-like penetration.

It took guts and skill and luck to survive. It took more than luck to live long enough to find a hunk of rock containing enough wealth to make it worth mining.

'Mass about fifty tons Earth weight. Size is small but that's because of the heavy metals. Osmium content . . . '

Redfern frowned as his fingers pressed the keys of the calculator. 'I'd guess about twenty per cent.' He looked at his partner. 'She's loaded, Murry. I told you that this was a big one!'

'Calm down.' Murry drifted forward and stared with pale eyes at the looming shape limned now by the stars, which it occluded. 'High density means tough mining. We need explosives, extra oxygen, gear we haven't got.' He swore with cold precision. 'It looks as though we've found ourselves a headache.'

'But . . . '

'Shut up! I . . . '

Both men winced as something slammed against the hull. The impact was followed by the shrill whine of escaping air, a screaming hiss as the precious gas streamed out into the void and Murry swore as he dived for a patch.

'That's the third time in ten days! Damn it, this section must be lousy with shrapnel.' He tore the soft, sucker-like rubber cup from a row on a bulkhead and slammed it over the hole. Internal pressure pressed it tight against the inner hull, sealing the punctured hull against such time as they could weld it whole again.

'Did it penetrate or explode on impact?' Murry stared around the control room. 'I've known one of those things to enter and blast the instruments to a heap of junk.' He sighed as he saw no damage. 'We were lucky, it must have been a small one travelling at high speed and it vapourised when it hit.'

Redfern stared at the older man, amazed at his calm acceptance of near-death, himself still trembling with thoughts of what might have happened. Speed had saved them. Air at thirteen pounds pressure was only too eager to stream into the void and any hole over a few millimetres in diameter would evacuate the ship almost at once. Not all the ship, of course, the bulkheads would see to that, the doors sealing off the rest of the vessel from the empty compartment, but that was no help when the break occurred in a section of the ship where there were men. Those men either sealed the hole or they died. Experience had taught them to seal the hole.

'Got it!' Murry snapped his fingers.

'Got what?'

'I know how we can have our cake and eat it.' Murry pointed towards the asteroid. 'Listen, can this tub haul that hunk of rock out of orbit?'

'Out of orbit?' Redfern looked blank. 'Why?'

'Don't ask stupid questions. Can it?'

'Yes. We could hook onto it and drag it after us if that's what you mean. Do you?'

'What else?' Murry scowled at the rubber patch against the hull. 'This section's too dangerous for mining anyway, we'd be riddled before a month was out, and we're low on oxygen as it is. We'll weld cables from the ship to the asteroid, blast off, and swing its orbit towards that of Mars.'

He mentioned it as if he were talking of taking a stroll and Redfern frowned as he mentally struggled with facts and figures.

'Wait a minute! That thing out there has high mass and even at full blast we couldn't move it very fast. Once we start it moving it's going to be the Devil's own job to stop. I . . . '

'Who said anything about stopping it?' Murry sneered his contempt. 'All we want to do is to get it out of orbit, saving it away from this sector and out into free space. What's so hard about that?'

'If you move it you'll disturb the orbits of other asteroids,' warned Redfern. 'They'll be so disrupted that they'll be unrecognizable.'

'So what?'

'But don't you see what it may mean? If we upset the balance between this and the others the disturbance will spread halfway around the Belt. Collisions will occur, main asteroids thrown off orbit, smaller ones sent running wild. What of the prospectors who may be caught? They won't know what's happening. All they'll know is that once-safe areas have suddenly become dangerous.' He shook his head. 'No, Murry, I can't do it.'

'You'll do it,' said Murry coldly. 'You'll do it because, if you don't, I'll kick you off-ship the very next time we land. This is my ship, remember? I've no time or room for a milksop. This is my chance to get rich and I'm taking it. Well?'

Redfern swallowed, knowing that he shouldn't agree, but nodding just the same.

Murry grinned.

★   ★   ★

Welding the cables was easy. Against the night of space the welding torches gleamed like trapped stars as the searing arcs caused metal to fuse to metal. Deftly they kicked themselves from asteroid to ship, from ship back to the asteroid, from asteroid to ship again, drifting like bloated fairies in the weightlessness of free fall.

Then came the hard part.

The ship groaned in every plate as the thrusting power of its tubes struggled to shift the immense mass of the captured piece of mountain. Twice the cables snapped and had to be repaired and augmented with other strands. Three times the engines had to be cut as the thin hand of the gauge crawled up and past the red danger area of fusing tubes. More than once Redfern shook his head at the rapid drop of the fuel gauge only to ignore it at Murry's insistence.

'We don't need fuel,' Murry snapped. 'Once we get well away from here we can always radio for a tug to bring us some. Keep trying.'

Finally they managed to swing the mass of the asteroid from its orbit and dragging it after them like a jagged ball on the end of a string, headed slowly towards the distant image of Mars.

And then they had time to think.

Redfern thought of Murry and Murry thought of Redfern, and both of them thought of the asteroid, which, like some ungainly monster speared in some alien sea, glided after the tiny bulk of the ship.

Redfern thought of his home and his friends and wondered what they would think of the company he kept. Murry was all right in his way, but his way was the prison way, the criminal way, the way of cold blood and hot temper, of calculated cruelty and murderous indifference. He was uncouth, low, foul-mouthed, content with a cheap woman and cheap wine, flashy clothes and the tawdry appurtenances of wealth. To such a man riches would do only harm — and anyway, he had found the asteroid.

Murry thought of the wasted years since he had been a boy, the years of struggle Redfern would never know. He thought of men he had shipped with, strong men some of them, dying as they clasped at dreams, ripped apart as they combed the Belt for the wealth it contained, finding it, only to be robbed and cheated, swindled and hoodwinked, shot and beaten up. He thought of himself twenty years ago. A young man then with an ideal and an aim. No education other than that given by the school of experience, no friends other than the assorted scum of a dozen ports, no hope except that offered by the eternal El Dorado of a lucky strike. What would Redfern, young fool that he was, do with so much money?

Money! Both thought about money. Osmium, ten tons of it maybe, and even at a credit the ounce that would mean over three hundred thousand credits. Platinum too, that was worth something, but the real money was in the osmium. A credit the ounce? That was the price of rough ore delivered to the combine. It was worth more, much more, but even at a credit an ounce it would mean a fortune.

Two fortunes, two small fortunes that is, one big one. Murry thought of money and hated the thought of sharing it with anyone. Redfern thought of money and begrudged his partner his share.

Both thought of murder.

Redfern thought of it and dismissed it immediately. Not murder. Murry was bad, rotten, greedy and criminal, but not murder. He couldn't do that.

Murry thought of it — and acted.

To kill was easy, to escape discovery was essential, and he knew just how to do both.

★ ★ ★

First he took the sealing patches from the sleeping cabin, all of them, lining them up

146

with the others on the control room bulkhead. They were well away from the Belt by now and the danger of being penetrated by meteors was so slight as to be negligible. Then he had to wait until the big man fell asleep. Not so easy this, a man didn't tire much in free fall, but sleep provided a welcome break in the monotony of shipboard routine. Then to test the door, centre swiveled and with extended overlap on either side so that, no matter which compartment was airless, the pressure on the other side would hold it immovable with all the force of thirteen pounds per square inch pressure. Then, with the seals removed, Redfern asleep, the door fastened against his waking, Murry donned his suit and, passing through the double doors of the air lock, emerged into space.

His plan was ridiculously simple.

It was so simple that it would work. Accidents happened, didn't they? They had been prospecting the Belt, hadn't they? Well then? With three normal punctures within ten days who could say why there couldn't have been four? It was bad luck, of course, that the sleeping compartment had been holed. Worse luck that Redfern had been asleep at the time. A tragedy that the door had sealed and that Redfern had obviously died before being able to stop the hole. A dead man, a scarred hull, a foolproof alibi — and ten tons of osmium, all his.

Murry grinned inside his helmet as he stepped cautiously over the outer hull.

He knew the vessel as well as he knew the palm of his hand, better, for he rarely examined the palm of his hand. He crouched over the section of the hull behind which lay the sleeping man, and the arc-torch in his gloved hand flared to instant life. A hole, not too big, with the seared edges and surround of meteor damage. The air would gush into space and, even if Redfern should awake, there was nothing he could do to seal the hole. Metal glowed as Murry lowered the torch.

After the air had escaped and Redfern was dead he would reseal the hole, normal procedure against which no one would complain. He would bleed air into the empty compartment, replace the patches, seal the room, evacuate it, and wait for the patrol and their investigation. With all decomposition arrested by the vacuum it would be impossible to find the true time of death. A perfect murder!

He chuckled again as the softening metal bulged a little from the internal pressure. He grinned as the searing arc of the welding torch vapourised the thin, outer skin. He laughed as he completed the hole.

And then he stopped laughing.

Air, confined at thirteen pounds pressure, blasted through the opening, slammed against his chest and sent him spinning and whirling away from the vessel. Driving him like a pea shot from some immense peashooter, his long, too long lifeline trailing behind him.

He had time for one scream as he saw the mass of rock and metal of the captured asteroid waiting to smash his faceplate into utter ruin.

Somebody didn't mind murdering in order to survive, Who?

NONENTITY

The lifeshell was a tin can with stores and a radio, an air conditioner and some accumulators, seven hundred cubic feet of space, a single direct vision port — and nothing else. It couldn't change course, land, orbit or spin. It couldn't do anything but drift, send out a radio signal and hope that some ship would receive it and come to the rescue. It had been designed to hold five people at maximum, and now it held seven. It was the slow route to hell with a preview thrown in for free.

The officer was a young man with a uniform ripped and soiled as though he had wallowed in muck and crawled through a hedge. One shoulder sagged lower than the other, his left arm was twisted and tucked inside his belt, and his face was taut with the pain from his broken bones. He sat on the stool before the radio equipment, his legs gripping the stem in a futile effort to remain in position, and stared at the six lives which, technically speaking, were in his charge.

'Would any of you be a doctor?'

They looked at each other, the three men, the two women and the boy, and their silence gave their answer.

'Know anything about first aid then?' The officer bit his lips against his agony. 'There's a medical kit . . . drugs . . . if you could dope me up?'

Again the looks, the blank expressions, the dragging silence as each waited for the other to move. Then the elder of the two women moved quietly towards the injured man.

Henley watched her, staring at her worn features, the lank hair, the body ruined by neglect and overwork. He knew her, a widow returning to Earth after wasting her life with a man who had been fated to fail before he started, then let his eyes flicker to the one stranger in the compartment.

The boy could have been no more than twelve, a pale, huge-eyed youth with the thin features and wasted appearance of those born in space. He huddled in a corner, one thin hand gripping a stanchion to hold him in position, and, staring at him, Henley wondered just who and what he was. An orphan probably, almost certainly now if not before, a waif, uprooted by war and flung among strangers. Idly he wondered how the boy came to be in the shell — the rest had all belonged to the same section — then forgot the boy as Rosina drifted towards him.

'Think he'll live?' It didn't take the jerk of the head to know whom she meant.

'Why not? We're in free fall, and a man can live a long time with serious injuries. Worried?'

'You kidding?' She licked her lips with a quick, almost feral gesture, and stared directly into his eyes. 'We're in trouble, buster, and don't you make any mistake about it. If pretty boy dies who's going to call for help?'

'Automatic radio call,' he said mildly. 'We don't really need him.' He kept his face blank at her expression of relief. 'Who's the boy?'

'That kid?' She shrugged. 'How should I know? Some poor devil separated from his people in the rush.' She shuddered at the memory of the past few hours. 'God! Who'd have thought people could act like that?'

'Panic,' he explained. 'Someone loses their head, fear gets out of control, it spreads, and before you know it you've a mob on your hands.' He looked up as a big man glided towards them. 'Jeff! How's your face?'

'I'll live.' The big man touched his slashed cheek. 'That wildcat nearly ripped out an eye. Damn crazy dame, why didn't she go to her own shell?'

'She didn't get in this one, anyway,' said Henley, dryly. 'You pack quite a right, Jeff. My guess is that you broke her jaw.'

'So what? When the chips are down only the strong can survive.' The big man dismissed the incident with a scowl. 'What's the matter with the old guy?'

'Prentice?' Henley stared up to where the third civilian drifted close to the small, round, star-shot port.

He was old and he was almost dead with fear. His hands trembled and his eyes had the glazed look of a man suffering from extreme shock. Little globules of spittle drifted from his quivering lips, his skin looked grey, and the sound of his breathing echoed horribly in the confines of the tiny compartment. Shock, terror, the sickening fear of imminent death and the physical frenzy of desperation as he had fought his way into the lifeshell had combined to bring him near madness and death. Time might cure him — if he were given time.

'What I want to know,' said Jeff, irritably, 'is what happened? All I remember is the alarm going off, the lights going out, and a lot of people screaming and yelling all around. I thought those ships were supposed to be foolproof.'

'The pile went, I think. I saw something explode as we blasted free.'

Rosina looked towards the officer. 'Would he know?'

'He should.' Henley pushed against the

wall. 'I'll go and ask him.'

The officer looked no better than he had before the first aid. Beads of sweat glistened on his face and neck, and his lips were grey instead of red. He looked up as Henley cushioned himself to a stop against the wall, then stared down at his equipment.

'Can I help?'

'Finished. Mrs. Caulder is quite a nurse.' The officer tried to smile at the woman. 'Thank you, madam.'

'I didn't do much,' she said, nervously. 'I'm not very clever at that sort of thing.'

'You did your best,' he said, quietly, then stared at Henley. 'I suppose you're wondering what all this is about?'

'Naturally, and so are the others. What went wrong?'

'Nothing went wrong, not in the sense you mean. We were sabotaged by the Numen.' The way he said it made the name sound like a curse.

'The Numen!'

'That's right. They must have sneaked one of their people aboard, God knows how or when, and he did a good job. First he spilled the pile then smashed the rod controls. He wrecked the lighting circuits and gimmicked the air doors. The guts of the pile burned their way towards the fuel tanks and touched them off. We blasted free only just in time.'

The officer winced as pain stabbed from his smashed bones. 'Damn fools! If they had only kept their heads we could have abandoned ship in good order. As it was, I had to fight my way to the shell and collected a few broken bones on the way.' He swore then, bitterly, savagely, more at the human animals who had reverted to the beast than at the saboteur.

'What happened to the Numan?'

'Dead, I suppose. Those fanatics consider a life well spent if they can take some of us with them, and this particular specimen really went to town. A ship and two hundred people, not to count the stores and equipment for the Mars base. We're lucky to be alive.'

'Are we?' Henley glanced at the terror-stricken figure of the old man. 'What are our chances?'

'No better and no worse than any other lifeshell ever blown adrift. If a ship picks up our call in time we'll be rescued.'

'And if it doesn't?' The girl thrust herself forward and Henley realized that everyone in the compartment had heard what the officer had said. 'How long must we wait to be picked up? That's what I want to know. How long?'

'Yeah.' Jeff joined the girl, one arm slipping possessively around her waist. 'When are we going to get out of this mess?'

'A few days, perhaps. Maybe a week or two. It depends.'

'And what if a ship doesn't arrive in time? What then?'

'Please!' The officer frowned at the girl and glanced towards the boy. 'There's no need to make things seem worse than what they are. Remember the child.'

'That's right.' Henley smiled towards the boy. 'What's your name, son?'

'Tommy, sir.'

'Well, Tommy, we're in a little trouble, but you mustn't worry about it. We're all going to be all right. Now you just do as you're told and you'll be home before you know it.'

'Yes, sir.' The boy hesitated. 'Sir?'

'Yes, son?'

'What about the others? My dad got left behind. Will he be home soon, too?'

'Of course.' Henley forced a false conviction into his tones as he patted the stringy black hair. 'Don't worry about it, Tommy, everything is going to be all right.' He looked at the toil-worn features of the woman. 'Perhaps you could take care of him, madam?'

'I'll look after him,' promised Mrs. Caulder. She pulled the boy towards her. 'Come on now, Tommy, time for you to get some sleep.'

Henley watched her as she mothered the boy, recognising a long thwarted maternal instinct in the way she touched him, smoothing his hair and resting his head on her shoulder. He turned as Jeff swore with quiet, bitter anger.

'The swine! The dirty stinking swine!'

'The Numen?'

'Who else? To do a thing like that. Wreck a ship in deep space and kill off

161

women and children as if they were vermin.' He knotted his big hands. 'If I could just get hold of the swine who did it . . . '

'He's dead,' said Henley, tiredly. He didn't want to get dragged into an argument on the merits of the war, and yet, deep within himself, he had a sneaking sympathy for the Numen. Whatever else they were, they were brave. They carried on a hopeless struggle with nothing to help them but their own courage and a fanatical determination to be left alone at all costs. Sometimes it was hard to remember that they were human, of the same stock as the Terrestrials, settlers who had carved a living from the hostile satellites of Jupiter, a living threatened by the occupation of those worlds by the advancing frontiers of civilization. Perhaps he would have felt different had he lost a wife or son in the wreck, but he hadn't and he was alive, and that was all that mattered.

Night came with the switching off of the light — to save power, though no one mentioned that — and in the heavy darkness seven people tried to forget worry and fear in sleep. It wasn't easy. Free fall didn't induce physical weariness, and the novelty and danger of their position tended to keep them all awake. Henley hooked one leg beneath the strut retaining the air tanks and stared into the darkness, listening to the various sounds sighing and ebbing through the heavy air.

A slobbering, half-baby, half-animal whimper, moist and drooling, sucking and horrible — the old man still living with his terror. A whispered croon — the woman soothing the child. A gasp and a hiss of indrawn breath — the officer with his broken bones. A murmur and a soft whisper — Jeff and the girl. A soft, mechanical drone — the whirling fan of the conditioner as it stirred the air.

He isolated and registered the sounds, identifying and locating the position of each. The officer was still at his radio, his legs gripping the stem of the stool. The woman and child were in the opposite, upward corner, the old man had drifted into the center of the cabin and Jeff and the girl rested beside the single door.

Seven people — with scaled rations for only five.

After a while the darkness and the heavy air, the lack of distraction and the murmuring silence brought a half-doze, half-coma, and he hovered in the strange region between sleep and waking, his thoughts flitting from one concept to another, touching lightly on old scenes and recent memories. Casually he thought of the war and of the saboteur who had died on his mission. He thought of the panic and the blue-lit hell of the last few moments when men and women had fought in the dim glow of the emergencies as they felt the spur of panic. He visualized his home and his office, the face of a woman he had once known, a friend and an enemy, the possibility of being picked up and whether or not the Numen would ever cease their fanatical struggle.

He snapped fully awake as he sensed someone at his side.

'Henley?'

It was the girl, breathing directly into his ear, the soft mass of her hair brushing his cheek as she hovered beside him. He waited a moment before answering, locating the heavy breathing of the big man where he drifted, finally asleep, almost seven feet above.

'Yes?'

'It's me, Rosina.' She gripped his arm and drew herself even closer. 'Look, you're intelligent, at least you can't be as dumb as that big ox. Maybe you could answer a question.'

'Maybe.' He kept his voice low, too, whispering directly into her ear.

'How much air and stuff does this shell carry?'

'Enough,' he said, carefully. 'Why?'

'Don't give me that,' she said, bitterly. 'I may be a cheap dancer working the dives, but I'm not stupid. Look, there're seven of us in here and there isn't room to spit. How long can the air and water and stuff last?'

'We carry scaled rations to last five people for a period of twenty-five days.' He wished that it were light so that he could see her expression. 'That answer you?'

'And how long will it take for us to be picked up?'

'I don't know. You heard what the officer said.'

'I want the truth, Henley, I'm a big girl now.'

'When the ship blew, a signal was broadcast on the emergency band. It will be received and the nearest vessel will head towards us. They will know the flight pattern of the ship, its velocity, the time of the explosion, and from that can work out just where we are. All they have to do is search until they pick up our signal.'

'How long?'

'They've probably received the signal already, but the nearest ship could be going away from us, so would pass it on. We'll have to wait until a ship can match velocities and, of course, they will have to get here from wherever they are.' He hesitated. 'I don't know how long it will take.'

'Days?'

'Highly unlikely.'

'Weeks?'

'Perhaps. Perhaps a month. It's impossible to say.'

'I see.' Against his ear he could hear the hiss of her indrawn breath. 'Rations for five and we're carrying seven. Six — the boy doesn't count. Say a month. Say . . . '

'If you're trying to work out what I think you are, I can give you the answer. Eighteen days.'

'I make it different.'

'Jeff uses a lot of oxygen and he's going to need a lot of water. He and the boy make two normal adults between them. Eighteen days.'

'And you said that we couldn't be picked up for at least a month.' Abruptly her fingers were digging into his arm. 'Henley! What can we do?'

'We?'

'Sure! Why not? The old guy's almost dead and the officer's well on the way. Jeff is dumb. Who have I left?'

'I don't like what you're saying,' he said, curtly. 'We're all in this together and I'm not going to be a party to killing anyone for their rations. I — '

'Killing? Who said anything about killing?' Despite the denial she didn't raise her voice. 'I never suggested — '

'Work it out for yourself,' he said, impatiently. 'The only way to stretch the rations is for someone to stop using them. I want no part of it.'

'You . . . ' For a moment he thought that she would strike him. Then she swore, thrust angrily at the metal and drifted away.

He shrugged.

The lights came on and they ate cold, tasteless paste from cans, washed down with stale water sucked through a nipple. Rosina ate in sulky silence, not looking at Henley, and after the meal drifted into a corner with Jeff, their heads bent close together. The woman moved towards the officer and Henley joined her as she opened the medical kit.

'How is he?'

'Bad. The collar bone is smashed and I think some ribs as well. His arm is useless and there's some internal bleeding.' She fumbled among the small store of drugs. 'There's nothing I can do.'

'Will he die?'

'I don't know. I hope not; he's such a nice young man and it's a pity that he should end like this.' There was a naked sincerity in her voice and Henley was surprised to find her eyes brimming with unshed tears. 'He reminds me of Joe, my husband, when we first met. That was back home before we left for the asteroids. I . . . ' She gulped and shook her head. 'You wouldn't be interested in that.'

'I could be interested,' he said, gently, and took the hypodermic from her hands. 'Let me do that.'

'Can you?'

'I can give an injection — if you tell me what to inject.' He glanced towards the boy, hunched against a wall, wide-eyed and shrunken. 'Go back to Tommy now, he looks scared.' For a moment mother instinct struggled with duty; then, as Henley turned towards the officer, her maternal feelings won and she returned to the thin-faced boy.

'How are you feeling?' Henley carefully slipped the needle into a vein and pressed the plunger. 'Better?'

'I suppose so.' The officer tried not to show his obvious pain. 'That stuff could be water for all the good it seems to be doing. How are the others?'

'Same as usual.' Henley wiped the hypodermic and replaced it in the medical kit. 'Prentice doesn't seem to be any better.'

'The old man?' The officer couldn't shrug, but his meaning was plain. 'He's had his turn. I'm more concerned with the boy. A hell of a fine way to start life. Those damn swine! I wish they were here now to see what they've done.' He gulped, his face a mask of sweat, and gestured for Henley to stoop closer. 'Look, I think that we'd better come to an understanding.'

'How do you mean?'

'I can't last much longer and the way I feel now the quicker I go the better I'd like it. Maybe it's just as well; we don't carry anywhere near enough stores for us all to last, and my share may mean life for someone.' He stared at Henley. 'I want that someone to be the boy. The rest of us are full grown and we've had our time, but the kid never had a chance. Understand?'

'Is it as bad as that?'

'Yes.'

'How long do you think?'

'Weeks, maybe. A month at least.' The officer swayed a little, and perspiration streamed from his contorted features. 'Don't kid yourself, Henley, this isn't going to be easy. Lifeshells are nice in theory. They can even be useful on the Tri-Planet runs, where space is full of ships and a one-week wait is the most expected. But we're a long way from the sun and space is a hell of a big place. Out here lifeshells are a morale factor; they're comforting to have around — so long as you don't have to use them. The rations are supposed to last twenty-five days, but that's all in theory, and as soon as you overload you're in trouble. That's another good reason why I'd better clock out pretty soon. While we're two extra the consumption goes up double.'

'Double!' Henley remembered to lower his voice. 'I don't get that. I made it that we could last eighteen days.'

'Excess humidity for one thing. Heat for another. We're not losing any heat, you know, just a little by radiation, and there are seven of us acting as quite efficient heat sources. The conditioner can't stand too much overload . . . carbon dioxide . . . non-conduction . . . ' The officer shook his head as he swayed again. 'The hell with it. I can't give you a lecture. Just remember what I said.'

Henley left him then, left him alone with his agony and the invisible burden of his responsibility, swaying and sweating from the pain of his torn tissues and crushed bones. And yet, despite his pain, the man could still think of the one thing that had made his race what it was. He could still think of the next generation.

Three days later he was dead, and those remaining faced a new problem.

There was no air lock in the lifeshell. The single door opened, if it were possible to open it at all, directly on space, and the refuse ejectors were far too small to permit of the expulsion of anything as large as a body.

'You'll have to get rid of him.' Rosina made a point of not looking at the silent figure, still sitting on the stool, the legs bound with a torn fragment of uniform. 'If I have to stay in here with that I'll go crazy!'

'Yeah.' Jeff automatically clenched his big hands as if the problem could be solved by physical violence. 'How do we do it, Henley?'

'We can't.'

'You've got to. I can't stand him sitting there like that! I can't stand it. I tell you!'

'Shut up, Rosina!' Henley stared at the big man. 'She's right, though. We can't leave him like that. In a couple of days he'll start going bad and you know what that'll mean.' He glanced at the others, the woman hunched against the boy, the old man still whimpering to himself as he wandered in the regions of his mental terror. 'As far as I can see it there are only two ways. We can seal him up in one of those big plastic bags in the locker, or we can pass him through the refuse ejectors. I suggest that we seal him up. I've an idea that is what those bags are for, and if we seal it, it should be airtight.'

'I don't like it,' protested the girl. 'Even if you seal him up he'll still be in here.

173

God! You think I want to keep company with a corpse?'

'What else can we do?'

'We could cut him up,' said Jeff, slowly. 'The ejectors would take small pieces and we could get rid of him that way.'

'You know what would happen then?' Henley stared bleakly at the big man. 'His blood would drift in tiny globules and break against whatever they touched. The human body holds quite a bit of blood, Jeff, and I don't think you'd like living under those conditions. A slaughterhouse would be hospital-clean in comparison.'

'But we'd get rid of the body.'

'Yes, and then we'd have to get rid of the blood.' Henley shook his head. 'We'll seal him up.'

'Who says so? I don't remember anyone making you the boss. Who are you to give the orders?'

'Do you want to give them?' Henley shrugged. 'Go ahead, then. Jam the ejectors and let our air escape into space. Fill the shell with blood and tissue then. When it goes bad, maybe you'll figure out a way to clean the air. Me? I don't give a

174

damn. If you want to act big in front of your girlfriend go ahead, but when you're spewing your life out two hours away from rescue, maybe you'll regret it.'

For a moment it hung in the balance. For a moment Henley thought the big man would react in the only way that seemed possible to a man of his type, with fists and boots, and blind, savage violence, then, to his relief, the big man blinked and nodded. 'We'll seal him up.'

The job didn't take long and Henley was glad of it. They pulled one of the two huge plastic bags over the body, sealed the edges, and fastened the shapeless bundle to a stanchion. Then they tried to forget it, tried to ignore the fact that it contained what had once been a man, and who, even though dead, still kept them company. Tried — and failed.

For death was too close. It hovered all around them, in the flickering needle of the air gauge, the falling hand of the power supply, the dwindling stores of food and water. Death rode the hands of the chronometer — and they all knew it.

And knowing it, they each reacted in

their own fashion.

Prentice did nothing. Lost in his mental world he drifted like a thing of wood, uncaring, unaware whimpering his animal sounds and twitching with his baby motions. The woman said nothing, but she clutched the boy a little more possessively, watched a little more sharply. The boy did nothing — merely watched and did as he was told, his wide, dark eyes and thin face a constant reproach to selfish thoughts. Jeff became a little more arrogant, a little too eager to grab his share of the rations, a little less polite and far more possessive. Rosina did something about it.

She came up to Henley one 'night', drifting like a pale ghost in the dim star-glow from the single port, and settled beside him where he sat on the stool.

'How are we going?' Again she whispered directly in his ear, her hair brushing against his cheek.

'As expected. Why?'

'You know what I mean. How long can we last now that the officer's dead?'

'About eight days.'

'Eight! How's that? With one less we

should be able to last a lot longer.'

'It isn't as simple as that. The overload cut down our time by half and the officer died too late to do us any good. I'd guess eight days, maybe ten, maybe seven. I don't know.'

'And the rescue?'

'At least twice as long.'

'So we're going to die.'

'Naturally. We've been going to do that since the day we were born.'

'Don't get clever with me, Henley, you know what I mean.' Against his ear her voice was surprisingly harsh and bitter. 'We're going to die . . . unless . . . '

'Unless what?'

'The old man's pretty useless,' she said, softly. 'He doesn't eat much, but he breathes a lot of air. Why should we all suffer to keep one worn-out old man alive?'

'Are you asking me, or telling me?' He stirred impatiently on the stool. 'You tried this once before, and my answer is still the same. We live or die together.'

'Why? Why should we consider others at all! It's our life, isn't it? We've only the one, and I intend hanging onto mine. If you weren't so damn noble you'd feel the same way.'

'Shut up!' He didn't trouble to lower his voice. 'I know your kind, Rosina. Selfish and rotten to the core. You've always had what you wanted and you've always managed to find some poor fool to get it for you. Now you want life, and you think I'll kill so that you can fill your lungs for a few days longer. Why should I? What the hell are you to me?'

'I'm a woman, aren't I?'

'So what? What's so special about being a woman? You think I'm like the rest of the morons you've met? Do you think I'd do anything for a woman merely because she is a woman? Get wise to yourself, Rosina. To me you're just a lump of flesh and nothing else. Remember that.'

'You — '

'Say that again and I'll smash your teeth down your throat. What's the matter, Rosina, won't Jeff play?'

'Go to hell!'

'We're all going to hell, one way or another.'

'You're a fool,' she said, bitterly. 'I'm not just talking of myself, there's others to consider — the kid, you, me. What is the old man to us? Nobility is all right in its place, but not here, not when we're racing the clock and losing out on every breath. If he died we'd all stand a chance.'

'We'd stand a better chance if Jeff died; he's big and uses too much air, radiates too much heat.'

'Leave Jeff out of this.'

'Sure, but if we're talking of survival, let's face the facts. You mentioned the old man, I mention Jeff. If they both were to die, maybe we'd stand a chance. The old man alone won't make any difference.'

'You wouldn't dare try to kill him.'

'Did I say anything about killing? You brought the matter up, not me, but suppose you got your own way and only the two of you were left. He's a big man, Rosina. I'd say that he uses twice as much air as you do, and he isn't particular how he gets it. Remember the way he hit that woman? If you were the last two alive, could you trust him?'

'I think so,' she said, uncertainly. 'He

likes me a lot, he wouldn't do anything to hurt me.'

'No?'

'No.'

'Then you've nothing to worry about, have you?' He stretched and smiled into the darkness. 'Forget it, Rosina. You're tired and worried. Better get some sleep now; things will seem better in the morning.'

She left him as silently as she had come.

With the morning came horror.

It came with 'day,' with the flashing of the single light, and it came with blood and violent death. Prentice was the one who died, his throat punctured and his blood spraying in a thick, red mist from the force of his slowing heart. Jeff was the one who hovered beside him, a knife in his hand, a foolish expression on his face, blood on his clothing and dull wonder in his eyes.

'He's dead,' he said, stupidly. 'The old man's dead.'

'So he is.' Henley felt his stomach muscles tighten as he stared at the big man. 'What made you do it, Jeff?'

'Do it? Do what?' Understanding and rage came together. 'I didn't kill him.'

'No?'

'Damn it! I tell you I didn't kill him and you can't make me say I did! I was asleep, drifting, and I heard a groan. I reached out and felt the knife and at the same time you put the lights on. Hell! Anyone could have done it!'

'Who?' Henley shook his head. 'You might have got away with it, Jeff, but you were unlucky. Another minute and you'd have been in the clear. You could have got rid of the knife, perhaps palmed it off on someone else, and the blood would have stained us all.' He took a deep breath. 'Sorry, Jeff, but the facts are plain.'

'Are they?' The big man closed his fist around the knife and glared his defiance. 'We'll see about that. I'm innocent and I know it, and when we get picked up the lie detectors will prove it. Someone in here is a murderer, and the only thing I'm certain about is that it isn't me.' He glared at the others. 'It could have been you, or Rosina, or the woman. How do I know that one of you didn't do it?'

'I was sitting here all night,' said Henley tiredly. 'Rosina?'

'I was with you part of the time, with Jeff some of the rest.' She didn't look at the big man. 'I was by myself just before the lights went on.'

'Mrs. Caulder?'

'Asleep. Tommy was restless and I didn't drop off for some time.'

'You see? No one's got an alibi. I just happened to be the unlucky one.' Jeff stared down at the dulled blade. 'Someone must have carried this thing on him, and it's not likely that it belongs to a woman. That leaves you and me, Henley — and I know that it wasn't me.'

'I didn't kill him,' said Henley, tiredly. He kicked himself from the stool. 'Talking is getting us nowhere. Let's seal him up and get him out of the way.'

They used the second and last of the big bags for the job, and lashed what remained of the old man beside the officer. They worked in silence, avoiding each other's eyes, and the sense of guilt and helplessness drove them apart as

soon as the job was done. Henley held
out his hand.

'The knife, Jeff. I'll take it.'

'I'm keeping it.'

'I want the knife, Jeff.'

'You can keep on wanting.' The big
man glowered his hate. 'And another
thing, the light stays on. I'm taking no
chances on getting stabbed in the dark.
Someone in here is a killer and I don't
intend to be the next. I'll keep the knife
for self-protection, and if you don't like
the idea, you can try to take it from me.'
He grinned, an animal writhing of the lips
devoid of humour. 'If you've got sense,
Henley, you won't try it.'

It was an ultimatum. It was defeat and
Henley knew it, and the knowledge was
bitter in his mouth. Angrily he returned
to the stool, then glanced up as Mrs.
Caulder drifted towards him.

'Mr. Henley.'

'Yes?'

'I'd like to talk to you.' She glanced at
the others and bent her lips to his ear.
'Privately.'

'Go ahead.' He bent his head, and like

183

two lovers, they sat cheek to cheek, each whispering into the other's ear.

'It's about Tommy,' she whispered. 'I'm worried about him.'

'There's no need to worry, Mrs. Caulder. It's a trying time for all of us, but he's young and he'll get over it.'

'I don't mean that,' she whispered. 'It's something else. I think . . . '

Her voice faded with the dying of the light, and in the sudden darkness Henley felt her stiffen and the sound of a curse.

'What the hell? Put those damn lights on!'

'I'm trying.' Henley fumbled for the switch, found it, flipped it without result. 'Must be fused.'

'Like . . . ' Jeff's voice cut off with a peculiar gurgle and something wet and warm sprayed Henley's face with sticky moisture. Desperately he fumbled at the unfamiliar wiring, tracing the strands from the switch to the fuses, feeling his way until current stabbed at his fingers with sudden pain. Gingerly he felt the wires, touched the severed ends together, and blinked in the sudden light.

'What happened?' Rosina was crouched in a corner, her face distorted with fear and terror, her skin dappled with tiny red patches.

'Someone cut the wires.' Carefully Henley twisted them together and frowned down at the join. He touched his face and stared down at his stained fingers. 'Jeff!'

The big man didn't answer. He couldn't answer, the knife thrust into his neck gave the reason and explained the red mist filling the compartment. 'Rosina! Are you all right?'

'Yes.'

'Mrs. Caulder!' Henley kicked himself towards the woman. 'Mrs. Caulder! Are you sick?'

She wasn't sick. She would never be sick again, and as she drifted a limp and inert bundle, her glazed eyes stared at the light with pathetic hopelessness, their expression matching the distorted angle of her head.

'Dead!' Henley gently felt at the thin neck. 'Broken; and someone killed Jeff.' He stared accusingly at the girl.

'It wasn't me, Henley. I swear that it

wasn't me.' She cringed at the murderous hate in his eyes. 'I stayed where I was when the lights went out. Henley! Don't look at me like that!'

'I can understand the old man,' he said, thickly. 'He was no loss to anyone. I can even understand Jeff, he would have been dangerous, but to kill the woman! To murder a decent, inoffensive woman whose only concern was for the boy. Damn you, Rosina, you've gone too far!'

'I didn't do it.' she pleaded. 'I didn't do it.'

'You cut the wires,' he accused. 'You saw your chance to safeguard that precious life of yours and you took it. Three dead and three to go. How long can we last now, Rosina? How long can we last now — damn you!'

Hate mastered him then. Hate and rage, and a sick distorted feeling of repulsion and murderous frenzy. She was strong but he was stronger, and even without weight he still had the greater mass. Her throat was slippery with blood by the time he gripped her, his hands were red with it, the entire interior was awash with sticky wetness, but it made no difference and he smiled as he watched her die. Afterwards, when he realized what he had done, he felt shame and guilt and a terrible feeling of revulsion.

'I'm sorry, Tommy,' he said, quietly. 'But she was a bad woman, you know that, and she had to die.'

The boy didn't answer. He sat as he had sat since the beginning, wide-eyed and silent, watchful and poised like an over-scared young animal, ready to run, but not knowing from where danger would come. Henley sighed as he looked at the boy, so young to have suffered so much, and, turning off the light, settled down to wait for rescue.

Somehow, it was better in the dark. It was better still when he finally drove himself to lash the drifting bodies to a stanchion, and even though the blood was a nuisance, it could be borne. He was safe. He was alive and the others were dead. He alone of them all would return to Earth and the warm comfort of civilization.

And he had a witness to prove his innocence.

He smiled as he thought about it; then, still thinking, he lost his smile. The officer had died a natural death, there was no mistake about that. The old man? Jeff. But Jeff had protested his innocence and held onto the knife. Mrs. Caulder had been touching him when the lights went out. Jeff had been talking to Rosina, so . . . who had cut the wires? And who had killed Jeff, big and armed and ready for trouble? And who had killed the woman, and why? She had died from a cunning blow to the neck, a skilled and highly technical blow unlikely to be known by the average person. Jeff could have done it, but Jeff was dying with a knife in his throat. Who?

'Tommy.' Henley tried to keep his voice calm and even. 'Where are you, son?'

'Worked it out yet, Henley?' The voice was the same, high and weak, and surprisingly boyish, but the tone was that of a man. 'Surprised? You shouldn't be. It was pretty obvious from the start.'

'You! You did it!'

'Of course.' The boy — it was hard to think of him as other than a boy — chuckled. 'I'm the saboteur you were all talking about. The scum you wanted to find and hurt. The filth you hate and despise because we're a little different from you and want to be left alone. You should learn more about your enemies, Henley.'

'So you're the Numan. You wrecked the ship and managed to get on this lifeshell.' Henley laughed, without humour. 'My God! And the officer died so that you could have his rations and a chance for life. You were the one we all felt sorry for. You!'

'The more fool you.' There was nothing but acid contempt in the young voice. 'I'm a Numan, yes, what you would call a midget, and I wrecked your ship and killed your people. Why not? We are at war, aren't we?'

'Then you must have cut the wires. You killed Mrs. Caulder and the others, but why? We meant you no harm.'

'The woman suspected, but even without that she would have had to die.

All of them had to die. You don't know much about survival, Henley. Jeff thought he knew, but he only played with the idea. To survive at all you have to be strong all of the time, not just a part of it. That's why we are going to win this war. We never stop, we daren't stop; for us the only rest and peace is in the grave.'

He paused, and in the silence Henley fumbled for the switch and tried to throw on the light. He wasn't surprised when nothing happened.

'I wanted the air and food in this lifeshell and to get it they had to die. You had the same idea, the girl, too, but you did nothing but talk. I didn't talk, I acted, and now I shall survive while the rest of you rot.' He chuckled again. 'Funny, isn't it? When the rescue ship arrives they will all be so sorry for the poor little waif without a home, the nonentity caught in the cross currents of war. They will look after me, take me to Earth, give me a home, and then . . . ' He sucked in his breath. 'Then I'll show them what their 'scum' can do.'

'Perhaps,' said Henley, softly, and

kicked himself to one side as steel lashed towards him. Savagely he struck out with the medical kit in his hand and grinned as he heard the knife tinkle against the plating. 'Now we're even, you little swine. Now we'll see who survives. You made a mistake, Numan; you talked too much, but then you couldn't help it, could you? Half-pints like you always like to brag.' Carefully he drifted across the compartment. 'We aren't really soft, you know, not anywhere near as soft as you like to think. We respect our children and ignore nonentities, but, once we know them for what they are, we haven't the slightest compunction at killing our enemies. I'm bigger than you, with more mass and greater strength, and I'm going to kill you — slowly.'

He drifted back across the cabin, feeling the sticky wetness on his face increase as he brushed against the hovering blood globules, and hate and rage, sorrow at what he had done to the girl, and anger at having been made a fool, all combined to fill him with a killing frenzy.

He didn't know that the air conditioner had stopped, clogged by the drifting blood, and that it was only a matter of time before he, too, would be dead.

It was pure coincidence that the two men met; such coincidences can, and do, happen. But if one coincidence, then why not another?

LINDA

If I hadn't broken my leg the whole thing would never have happened, but I did, and that's all there is to it. On Mars, naturally. Back home it wouldn't have mattered, it would even have had advantages, but things never seem to work out for me like that. Same as the time I went to Venus and fell into a mud hole. I could have picked one of the radiant, youth-giving springs, but instead of that I chose a stinking hole filled with gluey black mud. I went in up to my neck and the stench was awful. They wouldn't let me eat in the mess for a week, and there was even talk about shooting me to put me out of my misery. Some people have a peculiar sense of humour.

But about Mars.

I'd gone out into the desert looking for a snowflake. They aren't ice, of course — what little moisture there is hangs around the poles — but pieces of fantastically hard stone, weathered and fretted by the age-old winds and the sandblast effect of the dust into a delicate filigree of lace-like rock. Some of them are very beautiful, all are different, and most are quite valuable. I'd been trying to find one for years now. Each time I landed on Mars I'd spend the three-day stop over wandering over the desert hoping to see one sticking out of the dust. I never was lucky and you need a lot of luck to find one, but I kept hoping.

Until I broke my leg.

The doctor shook his head when he saw it, and Hanson, the waspish dispatcher, snorted as he realized what had happened.

'You fool, Carter,' he snapped. 'Now you'll have to stop over until the next ship.'

'No.' I sweated at the thought of it. 'I'll be all right. The doc can fix me up with Stader splints and I can take it easy on the way back.' I looked hopefully at the medic. 'It will have healed by then, won't it, doc?'

He shook his head.

'You've got a nasty compound fracture

there, and it needs attention. Take-off's in a few hours and you'll never be ready in time, even if I allowed you to go, which I won't.'

'Why not?'

'A pilot needs two legs,' he said. 'If he loses one, then he's no longer a pilot. Is that what you want?'

'Is it as bad as that?'

'It is. The broken ends of the bone have slashed the tissue pretty badly and the shock of takeoff may just about ruin what's left.' He shrugged. 'Take it easy, Carter. You're not going anywhere for a while.'

Which was pretty definite.

I scribbled a note to Linda and gave it to Hanson just before he hurried out to break the news to the rest of the crew that they would have to do without me on the way back home. They could manage, of course; a rocket ship can be handled by two men instead of three, but it wouldn't be easy, and it meant constant watches with little off-time. I called to him just as he had opened the inner door of the hospital ward.

'Don't forget to make a place for me on the next ship back.'

'Relax,' he snapped. 'You'll have to wait until they send for you.' The door slammed after his thin figure, and I stared bleakly up at the low ceiling.

I felt sick. It wasn't the pain, though that was bad enough, it was knowing just how long I was going to be stuck here. The round trip took three months with a three-day stopover at each end. That gave me a maximum of twelve days a year on Earth, and now, owing to my missing the return trip, I was going to lose three of those days.

And I'd only been married six months.

★   ★   ★

I didn't hear the ship leave. They had me in the operating theatre by then, fixing my leg with the metal Stader splints, riveting them on the broken bone so that I wouldn't need external splints or plaster. I didn't mind that so much, and at first I didn't mind the waiting in the ward while the damaged tissues mended. I spent a lot of time reliving my first meeting with Linda, what we had said and done, what we were going to say and do.

I liked that especially.

I had a photograph of her, a small, head and shoulders picture, tinted and glossy. It wasn't too good a likeness, but it did show her blue eyes and blonde hair fluffed in the latest style. She seemed to be smiling at me, a warm, intimate smile, and staring at it I felt like getting up and walking back home. Six days with a wife to whom you've only been married six months isn't long enough to get indifferent. In a way our honeymoon hadn't even started, and as far as I was concerned it would never finish.

That's the trouble with space pilots. They're too much alone, and each of us has a hell of an inferiority complex. They pick us because we're small, slight, boyish. That way we don't need much food or water, less air and take up little of the pay-weight. But most of us wish that we were different. It isn't nice to be among others, big men and tall, broad shouldered and strong. Not on a dance floor or at a party where you can see the girls eyeing the big ones with wistful longing.

It's things like that which make a man value a wife if he can get one.

I was lucky. Linda and I seemed to go for each other, and when I'd plucked up courage to ask the important question she'd said yes. For me it was third time lucky. Twice before I'd tried to get a permanent girl of my own, but each time I'd been turned down. My pay was good, sure. I wasn't home much — and that could have its advantages. But I was a space pilot, small, neurotic, and, for a woman who wanted a normal life, I and those like me were a dead loss.

That's what made Linda so important to me.

After the first couple of weeks they let me get up and hobble around. At the end of the first month they found me a job, some routine thing where I wouldn't get in the way but could earn my food and water. I tried to find a snowflake again. Linda wanted one, but I'd had my warning and didn't take any chances. I walked a little, worked a little and thought a lot.

I thought about Linda.

When I was stronger I applied for, and got, a change of work. I had mechanical knowledge, all pilots must have, and so I set about stripping and tuning the big, turbine-motored desert vehicles. The work was easy and left me plenty of time to think.

So I thought about Linda.

Time crawled past like a broken-winged butterfly, day after day, routine job after routine job, and in between wondering how the colonists stood it without blowing their tops, I thought about Linda. I dreamed about her, saw her face in every dune and reflecting surface, damn near made myself sick thinking about her, and by the time the rocket ships came I was about ready to scream with sheer wanting and need.

* * *

They'd sent two ships and I was in the dispatcher's office before the jets had had time to cool. Hanson glared at me. I couldn't blame him, what with haunting him to find out when the ships were due and telling him about Linda he had grown to hate the sight of me. He spoke before I could ask the inevitable question.

'Relax, Carter. They've sent for you.'

'Good.'

'Yeah, you're damn right. Much more of you and I'd have tied a rocket on you and sent you off.' He grinned. 'You're to go back with Landry. He and you will operate as a two-man crew and the other ship will take on the extra man.'

'Did they send them out with short crews, then?'

'Yes.' He shook his head. 'Damned if I know why pilots are so scarce. They must be running out of midgets or something.'

I didn't let it annoy me.

Landry was an inch taller than me, with a wide, humorous mouth and glinting blue eyes. He shook hands with me and raised an eyebrow.

'What the hell have they been doing to you, Carter? You look as if you'd just lost your last cent.'

'That sourpuss always looks like that,' grunted Hanson. 'The trouble with him is that he doesn't know how to be cheerful.' He grinned. 'Better do what you can for him on the way back, Landry. If he arrives like that, that wife of his will take off for a bit of extra-marital cheering up.'

'Cut it out,' I said.

'Listen to the guy!' The dispatcher shook his head. 'Doesn't he know the facts of life yet? What does he think the little woman's been doing all the time he's been stuck up here? Knitting?'

He really laughed then, and I felt the slow burn of rage. One of the penalties of being a pilot is that, after a few trips, you're not so good a man any more. The radiations in space turn you sterile, so any joke about parenthood is more than in bad taste. Even Landry looked uncomfortable.

'Shut your big, fat mouth,' I snarled, and stepped towards the grinning dispatcher. 'That isn't funny.'

'No?' He wiped his eyes. 'Maybe not, from where you're standing, buster. But you should be where I am.'

I hit him then, swinging wildly and burning with anger because I couldn't hurt him. He dodged and caught my arm, still grinning, and picked me bodily off the floor.

'Now, now, little man. Mummy spank.'

I almost cried with temper. The low gravity helped, of course; he couldn't have picked me up the way he did without it, but that didn't make any difference. He grinned at Landry.

'I wonder what his woman would think of him if she saw him now?'

That did it. I couldn't hurt the big oaf by sticking to the rules so I stiffened my fingers and jabbed him in the eye. He yelled like a stuck pig, dropping me to the floor, and clapping his hand over his face. Landry caught my arm.

'Let's get out of here,' he ordered. 'Quick.'

★　★　★

I hadn't blinded the dispatcher, not quite, but he glared at me with his unbandaged eye as we checked out and I knew that he had something to remember me by. I let Landry handle the take-off, sitting by the gyros and aligning the ship as he squinted through the instruments and called out the corrections. Finally, we both settled down as he fed power to the main burners and built up velocity for the long, powerless flight back to Earth.

Then impatience shook me so that I could have beaten my head against the bulkheads.

I was going home, but it was still a long way away, and, now that I had actually started, I was in a fever of impatience to get there and to see Linda again.

'You know,' said Landry one day. 'This is a funny kind of life. I've met a lot of fellows and everyone seems to do it different. Some get married, others take what they can where they find it, and some just act like monks.' He stared at me. 'You're married, aren't you?'

'That's right.'

'I'm not.' He grinned, a smug, tom-cat grin. 'No need to.'

'No?' I said.

'No,' he said, and that started it.

A spaceship isn't very big and it is important that the crew members get on well together. Usually with a three-man crew it isn't too hard; there is a fresh viewpoint, another personality, and if you don't like one man you can get on with the other. I think that's the main reason for a three-man crew. Some funny things happened in the early days when weight was so important that they had to cut down to a minimum.

Landry had a kink. Nothing too bad or nasty, but he was woman crazy. I've seen it before; the reaction of a very small man is usually to get very pugnacious or very self-conscious. Either extroverted or introverted. If the former he wants to prove that he is every inch a man, and the way Landry did it was to prove that he could get the girls.

And, of course, he had to talk about it.

* * *

Even discounting half of what he claimed and taking the rest with a pound of salt, he was still quite a boy. According to him

206

he needed every moment between stop-overs to recover from his dissipations, and the girls were lined up at every spaceport just waiting to fall into his arms. Privately I thought that he was a liar. In my experience men who do, don't talk about it, and those who'd like to but don't talk too much. Even so, I had to listen and after the second week Linda had become more important to me than ever before.

' . . . So she suggested we go up to her place where she had a bottle and I tagged along.' He smirked. 'Her sister was there, a lush dish and, believe it or not, those two females wouldn't give me a minute's rest . . . '

I grunted something and wished that we were travelling twice as fast. I pretended not to pay attention, deliberately ignored his half-hearted questions, grinned with what I hoped was open disbelief, but it didn't stop him. Nothing would have stopped him. I was an audience.

' . . . I'd just stepped off the ship when this red-haired dame called to me. She had a big car and lots of money, a film star I think. Boy! I don't think I slept for three days, and when it was time for take-off I had to be helped up the ladder . . . '

On and on, day after day, lie after lie, until I felt like twisting his neck.

' . . . A blonde dish. Married of course, and what her old man was missing! Said she liked me because I was small; same reason why she got married to a little guy, mother instinct, but there wasn't anything motherly about the way . . . '

Red head, brown head, blonde and brunette. White, dark, yellow Terrestrial, Martian Cabaret girls, call girls, matrons. Sisters, wives, daughters. Women. Women! Women! Nothing but lying tales of his damned women. And I had to listen.

Finally, in desperation, I talked back. I told him of Linda, of what she meant to me and what I meant to her. How we had met and what we had done. How I missed her and the plans I had made. I spilled it all out and he listened, half-impatiently, half-pityingly, and when I had dried up he shook his head.

'Marriage,' he said, and I didn't like the

way he said it. 'That's not for guys like us. We're away too long and when the cat's away . . . ' He smirked. 'Look at me now. I'm not married, but brother, do I regret it? Not on your life. I can get any one of twenty women, and change each time I feel like it. No worries about what they're up to when I'm gone, no paying to keep a book for someone else to read, or an apartment for someone else to share. No, sir! I'm smart.'

'It's not the same,' I protested. 'Those clippies you pick up are only after your cash.'

'So what?' He shrugged. 'And you're wrong at that. I'm a glamour boy, a space pilot, and they're curious to see what makes me tick.' He winked. 'Catch on?'

'No,' I said firmly. 'It's not the same as having a wife of your own.'

'You say that because you're scared.' Landry grinned to take the sting from his words. 'You're the sort of a guy who has never had a lot of girls. Now you've got one, you want to hang onto her, so you marry her, and then make the mistake of putting all your hopes into her hands.

What if she lets you down?'

'She won't.'

'How can you be sure?' He grinned at my expression. 'I'm not talking personally, you understand, but I've seen it happen. A quiet, self-conscious guy like yourself gets married and builds his whole life on his wife. He lives for her, works for her, almost grovels at her feet. He worships her, can't think of anyone but her, and when she lets him down . . . ' He made a gesture with his hands. 'Wham! End of pilot.'

'You're crazy.'

'Not me, boy. I'm smart. I keep my heart and if one of them brushes me off, what the hell? I can always find another. Like Linda for example.'

'Linda?'

'Sure. A dame I met in New London a few months ago.' He grinned. 'Nice.'

I swallowed, trying to control the sudden pounding of my heart. Linda lived in New London, we had set up home there after we were married. Could this swine..? I shook my head. Impossible. Lots of girls were named Linda; the famous woman pilot of generations ago had bequeathed her name to countless offspring and it was certain that more than one of them lived in New London . . . But?

'What about her?'

'Nothing much. I'd been hoping to meet a friend of mine, a red-head dancer, and she didn't turn up. I was feeling a bit low when this woman ran up to me and threw her arms around my neck.' He grinned. 'Mistaken identity; she'd thought that I was her husband, it was getting dark and it happened at the spaceport.'

'So?'

'So she wasn't as upset at the mistake as she could have been. In fact she wasn't upset at all.'

'I see.' I fought to keep my voice normal. 'What was she like? This girl you met.'

'Linda?' He shrugged. 'About six inches taller than me, blonde, blue eyes.' He made gestures with his hands. 'Figure about . . . so. Warm blooded, too, and . . . ' He caught sight of my expression. 'What's the matter?'

'Nothing.' I gritted my teeth and swallowed something that threatened to choke me. 'What happened?'

'Between me and Linda?' He looked smug. 'Be your age, pal, you're a big boy now.'

'Yes,' I said, and stared hard at the bulkhead. 'Of course.'

I left him then, afraid to show my feelings, and spent a lot of time tinkering with the gyroscopes a job that didn't need doing but took me out of range of Landry's voice and gave me time to think.

Linda and that swine — lovers?

I couldn't believe it, I didn't want to believe it, and yet..? The name was the same, the town, the general description. With Landry operating a different schedule to me, the meeting could have happened as he described and normally, I'd never know. She could have had other such meetings with other men and, while each of us kept flitting like clockwork on our rigid schedules between the planets, isolated from each other and all gossip, we would never know.

But I wasn't worrying about the others.

I was worrying about me. I'd married her.

If only I could be sure.

I clung to that like a drowning man clinging to a straw. Coincidence played some funny tricks and, anyway, I trusted her, sure I did, but . . . There was always that 'but'. I sweated at it while tinkering with the cold metal. If Landry had seen her during one of his stopovers back on Earth then I must have been away. I'd never seen him before. Nothing strange in that. I'd not seen hardly any of the other pilots, and few of them had seen me. Now, if he had met her at the spaceport and she had been expecting to meet her husband, could it have been Linda? Or, I swallowed as I thought about it, could he have met her after she had just seen me off?

Somehow, that made it even worse.

* * *

I stood it as long as I could, while worry tore at my guts and doubt turned my spine to mush, and when I couldn't stand it any longer I went upstairs to the control room. Landry gave me a queer look as I drifted through the hatch. I must have reflected something of what I was feeling in my face, and for once he didn't immediately break into another boastful story of his conquests. I didn't waste time.

'This woman you were telling me about, this Linda. What was her other name?'

'I don't know; she never mentioned it and I didn't ask.'

'Oh? When did you first meet her then?'

'A few trips back.' He shrugged. 'What's the matter, Carter?'

'Matter?' I forced myself to grin. 'Nothing. Nothing at all, just interested. Maybe I know her.'

'I doubt it, a female like that?' He shook his head. 'Not you, boy, you're decent.'

'Still,' I insisted. 'You can tell me about her, can't you?'

'Sure.' He gave me that tomcat grin. 'Getting ideas, son?'

'Maybe.' I tried to return his grin and

he seemed to ease a little. I wasn't surprised. A man like that has a mind that runs strictly on one track and finds it difficult to imagine that others could be different. 'What was she like?'

'I told you. Blonde, blue-eyed, soft and warm, and with a figure straight from the advertising hoardings. No artificial aids there, boy.' He chuckled. 'I know.'

'Did you ever meet up with her husband?'

'Are you serious? What would I want to meet him for?'

'I meant by accident. You said that he was a space pilot; you could have bumped into him.' I tried to keep the tension from my voice. 'It shouldn't be hard to guess who he is; he must have left the same time as you landed.'

'You could be right,' he admitted carelessly. 'But what the hell? Who gives a damn who he might be? What he doesn't know won't hurt him.'

'What was the date, Landry?'

He stared at me, not answering, and watching him I saw his expression alter. Not much, just a tightening of his lips and a slight narrowing of his eyes, an impression of wariness and alertness, nothing more. I repeated the question.

'What was the date?'

'I forget,' he muttered. 'What's it to you, anyway?'

'Maybe nothing.' I fought to control my voice. 'But surely you remember the date you first met her?'

'No.'

'You damn liar! You filthy, gloating swine!' I had lost all control now. 'You know what I'm getting at. What was the date?'

He recoiled from me, pressing his body hard against the smooth metal of the bulkhead, thrusting against it as though he hoped he could pass through the thin metal.

'You're crazy,' he muttered. 'What are you getting at?'

'You know damn well what I'm getting at.' I felt spittle wet my chin and the muscles along the edge of my jaw ached. 'You know damn well who Linda's husband is. Me! Me, damn you! Me!' I was shouting and within me something

216

bubbled and seethed as it clamoured for release. Landry turned white.

'No! You're wrong, Carter, I swear it! Lots of ships take off and land, and she could have stayed on to watch them. You're wrong, I tell you, you're wrong!'

'Am I?' I thrust the photograph in front of his eyes. 'Look! Blonde, blue eyes, about the right height, married to a space pilot, living in New London, and named Linda! Look at her, damn you! Look at her!'

I saw his eyes flicker to the colour print, then back to stare into my own eyes.

'Soft and loving, warm and lonely, likes small men and well stacked.' The words seemed to be ripping my insides to shreds, but something inside of me forced them past my lips. 'Cuddlesome wasn't she? Loving? You liked that didn't you, you filthy swine. You thought it funny, a joke, something to brag about. You . . .'

'No! No, Carter! No!' He cringed against the bulkhead. 'You're wrong. That's not her, not her, I tell you. Not . . .'

I smashed his skull, slamming the wrench I had taken from the tool rack by the gyroscopes hard against the bone, feeling something yield beneath the blow. I put everything I had into it, making up for lack of weight by muscle and mass, and the alloy tool dug deep into his brain. Blood spurted from the wound, driven by his heart, and with the blood something grey and nasty oozed around the wrench. The grey stuff stayed where it was, but the blood sprayed in a mist of tiny drops, drifting about the control room and spotting my face and hands where they touched, breaking their surface tension with the contact.

It was only then that I realised what I had done.

Not that I regretted killing Landry; the foul-mouthed swine had deserved it, and I'd only been the instrument of justice, but it left me in a spot. I thought about it as I stared at the dead man still pressed against the bulkhead the tool still buried in his stupid skull, his dull eyes still glaring at me. I thought about it, then drifting over to one of the acceleration chairs, I sat down and thought about it some more.

I had to get rid of the body, but even that was a crime in itself. The regulations were very simple. Any dead man had to be put in his spacesuit and returned to port. No spatial burials; that pleasant custom had led to too many mysteries, too many convenient disappearances. Two men would set out and one return. His explanation? His friend had died and he'd had to evacuate him into space. Nice and clean, no bodies, no questions, nothing but a gold-plated opportunity to murder.

Or so the legislators had thought, especially as there was no reason whatever for any crew member to leave the ship, and now to return without a full crew, dead or alive, was automatically assumed to be proof of murder.

I couldn't kick Landry into space.

The more I thought about it the worse it seemed. I'd killed Landry. He'd deserved it, but I didn't want to die for killing a louse. For the first time I regretted the method I'd used; a smashed skull wanted some explaining when most of the trip took place in free fall. I was still thinking about it when I swung into orbit for landing.

★   ★   ★

The stay on Mars had made me a little rusty, or maybe there were other reasons, but I came down hard, too hard, slamming the fins against the flame-scorched concrete with a jar that twisted members and brought the crash trucks whining from their sheds. I yelled to them from the open port at the nose and white-coated figures scrambled up the ladder towards me.

Mutely I led them inside the ship.

'Landry hadn't strapped down and the shock of landing flung him forward against the control panel.' I swallowed. 'I'm afraid that he's dead.'

'Dead?' One of the doctors pushed past me and stooped over the body. He pursed his lips as he examined the top of the crushed skull and stared thoughtfully at the grey-red smear on the once-bright panel. 'I'll say that he's dead, the entire

220

skull has been splintered.' He looked at me. 'How come?'

'I brought her down. I was out of practice, or maybe I misjudged, I don't know, but I cut the jets too soon and almost wrecked the ship.' I shuddered. 'He didn't stand a chance. I was a bit dazed from the shock and when I saw what had happened . . . '

'Nasty,' agreed the doctor. He stood by while a couple of interns wrapped Landry in a rubber sheet and lowered him from the nose port. Another man, a port official, moved casually about the ship, looking at this and staring at that. Once he stopped by the smear and touched it, staring at his finger before wiping it on his handkerchief.

I tried not to look at him.

'Have any trouble during the trip, Carter?' He didn't look at me when he spoke. I shrugged.

'No.'

'Sure?' This time he did look and I wished that he hadn't. I was never a good liar.

'Nothing particular.' I snapped my

221

fingers. 'I had a touch of nose bleed, nothing serious but it messed things up a bit.'

'I noticed that.' He rested his finger on a tiny red spot on the bulkhead, a rusty brown spot flaking a little as the blood dried. 'Anything else?'

'How do you mean?'

'Personal trouble. Landry wasn't the easiest sort of man to get on with, talked too much and talked too often.' He stared at me. 'Any fights?'

I shook my head, guessing that the dispatcher on Mars must have reported what had happened when I'd stabbed at his eye. The psycho-boys would have pursed their lips over that and checked the compatibility records of both Landry and myself. They had to be careful how they mixed the crews.

'Can I go now?' I moved carelessly towards the ladder. 'I've been away a long time and my wife will be waiting for me.'

'Just a second.' He touched the smear again and looked slowly around the room. 'You say Landry died a few minutes ago, just when you landed?'

'That's right.'

He nodded, and sauntered over to the locker where the bottled water and enriched soup which passed as food was stored. He stared at the ranked containers then examined the air-tank gauges. By that time I'd almost given up.

'I felt a bit sick on the way in,' I explained. 'Didn't eat much and went easy on water.'

'Did you cut down on breathing, too?' He took my arm and his fingers felt like chilled steel. 'Want to tell me about it?'

'About what?'

'Don't you know?'

I knew all right and cursed myself for the fool that I was. Rocket ships operate on a strict pay-weight schedule, and air, food and water is rationed down to the last ounce. Even if I could get by with the excess of food and water, it would be hard to account for the extra air left in the tanks — and Landry had died ten days ago.

'We'll find out,' he said quietly. 'It was a mistake putting you two together in the first place, but that doesn't excuse what happened. You may as well confess, Carter. Once the lab boys get through with examining the body we'll know almost to the hour just when he died — and it's a pretty safe bet that he's been dead longer than you claim.' He left me at the top of the ladder. 'I wouldn't jump, it's not worth it.'

I climbed down the metal rungs. Strangely I didn't feel anything but relief that it was all over. Living with a dead man for the past ten days had done something to me and I still squirmed at the memory of what I'd had to do just before swinging into orbit.

It hadn't been nice.

Linda met me at the gate, stepping forward to throw her arms around my neck and give me the big kiss I'd dreamed of for the past six months, the kiss I couldn't take. She stepped back, her eyes hurt and brimming with tears.

'John! What's the matter?'

'Ask your boyfriend,' I said bitterly. 'If you can.'

'No need for that, Carter,' said the man at my elbow. 'She's your wife.'

'Like hell, the no-good tramp ... ' I would have said more but I was interrupted.

A woman came pushing through the crowd, a washed-out blonde with old, tired, once-blue eyes. Her figure was generous, and to call it that was being kind. She was about five inches taller than I was, and youth was something she had long forgotten. She pulled at my sleeve.

'Please, mister. Where's Landry?'

'Landry?'

'Yes.' She simpered. 'My boyfriend; didn't he tell you about me? I'm Linda.'

They must have wondered why I laughed.

THE END

We do hope that you have enjoyed reading this large print book.

Did you know that all of our titles are available for purchase?

We publish a wide range of high quality large print books including:
Romances, Mysteries, Classics
General Fiction
Non Fiction and Westerns

Special interest titles available in large print are:
The Little Oxford Dictionary
Music Book, Song Book
Hymn Book, Service Book

Also available from us courtesy of Oxford University Press:
Young Readers' Dictionary
(large print edition)
Young Readers' Thesaurus
(large print edition)

For further information or a free brochure, please contact us at:
Ulverscroft Large Print Books Ltd.,
The Green, Bradgate Road, Anstey,
Leicester, LE7 7FU, England.
Tel: (00 44) 0116 236 4325
Fax: (00 44) 0116 234 0205

*Other titles in the
Linford Mystery Library:*

DEATH IN THE SQUARE

Ardath Mayhar

The upper-class inhabitants of the locked-gate community called Holroyd Square in Templeton, Texas are used to their sedate, private lives — and the equally private dark secrets that each of them keeps hidden from the others. But when a vicious blackmailer rudely interrupts their existence, and is then found murdered in the Square, the police must be called. Now only Assistant Chief Wash Shipp can uncover the killer and save their tattered reputations . . .

THE SECRET ENEMY

Manning K. Robertson

It is the height of the Cold War. British Agent Steve Carradine's mission is to locate and smuggle to the West a defecting Russian scientist with the vital secret of a new technology — but the Soviets are hot on his trail. Aided by a mysterious female agent, Carradine finds Professor Ubyenkov, and the three fugitives make a desperate flight on the Orient Express in a superhuman effort to remain alive and escape to Britain.

MURDER ON ICE

Paula Williams

After her boyfriend runs out on her with the contents of their joint bank account, Kat Latcham has no choice but to return to the tiny village of Millford Magna where she grew up. The place, she complains, is not so much sleepy as comatose, and she longs for something exciting to happen. But when she and her childhood friend Will discover a body, and Will's father is suspected of murder, Kat suddenly realises she should have heeded the saying, 'Be careful what you wish for'.

MR. WHIPPLE EXPLAINS

Gerald Verner

Mr. Augustus Whipple spends most of his time reading detective stories and thrillers. And his hobby stands him in good stead when he is faced with crimes in real life, for his fictional experiences enable him to find a solution to two mysterious murders, which comes as a surprise to the police and his next door neighbour, Inspector Gallers of Scotland Yard. And Gallers has particular reason to be grateful for Mr. Whipple's hobby when he finds himself arrested as chief suspect for the second murder . . .

THE SUBSTANCE OF A SHADE

John Glasby

Soon after moving into Mexton Grange, an old Georgian country house in the Cotswolds, Alice hears disquieting stories and rumours about her new abode: the previous owners had been driven out by a strange, oppressive atmosphere in the house. It was not as if the house was *actually* haunted — rather, it was as if the house was *waiting to be haunted* . . . These five stories of terror and the macabre by John Glasby will tingle the spine on any dark and stormy night.

THE GLASS HOUSE

V.J. Banis

When Antoinette swindled Margaree out of the old estate on Cape Breton Island, Margaree swore on her mother's grave that she'd win it back. But blocking her ambition are three deadly obstacles: the formidable Antoinette; her treacherous son; and Jean, whom she loves deeply but who hates the old house with all his heart. To win Jean, Margaree would have to give up the estate. The key to it all lies somewhere within the mysterious reaches of the Glass House . . . if Margaree remains alive long enough to find it!